D1231770

THE HUNDRED-YEAR MYSTERY

A treasure in jewels and gold coins is hidden somewhere on the Beacon College campus! But where is it? And where is the codicil in which John Beacon, founder of the school, revealed its location?

These are the questions the Danas are asked to resolve by their uncle, Phil Kenmore, president of Beacon, as the college approaches its centennial, the date on which it is to receive the fortune.

During their investigation, Louise and Jean explore spooky caves and are almost drowned at the site of a Viking mishap many centuries ago. But even before their hunt begins, the Danas are harassed by extortionists who claim to have the missing codicil. The girls' efforts are sabotaged over and over again by these unscrupulous enemies who will use any means—even the bombing of the school—to terrorize the Danas and hamper their search.

Their resolve unshaken, the Danas follow every lead until, through a study of ancient Viking symbols and customs, they outwit their enemies in a breath-taking finale.

"It's a real skeleton!" Paul exclaimed.

The *Dana Girls* Mystery Stories

THE HUNDRED-YEAR MYSTERY

By Carolyn Keene

GROSSET & DUNLAP
A FILMWAYS COMPANY
Publishers • New York

CONTENTS

THE
HUNDRED-YEAR
MYSTERY

CHAPTER I

A Sudden Attack

"You girls are always gadding off to solve a mystery," said Ken Scott, who was tall, slender, and blond. "I hoped we'd see more of each other before going back to school."

Louise and Jean Dana laughed, and Jean added, "I plead guilty to solving mysteries, but it's fun."

"And exciting," said Louise. "You boys are invited to come and help."

"We'll be there," said Chris Barton, who was dark-haired and loved to joke. "What's the mystery?"

"It's a hundred-year-old puzzle that has something to do with the Vikings."

The four young people were seated in the attractive living room of the Dana home.

"You said Vikings?" Ken repeated. "Weren't they the first known white men to set foot in America?"

"Yes," Louise replied, then said that the president of Beacon College and his wife had invited them to go there and solve the mystery.

"Tell us more about it," Chris begged.

As Louise went to a desk to get the letter, she explained that Dr. Kenmore was her uncle, the brother of the girls' deceased mother.

"Read the message aloud," Jean suggested.

"All right," her sister agreed, "but first I must tell you about something intriguing. Uncle Phil says that the hundred-year-old mystery must be solved before the centennial celebration of the college this fall."

She turned back to the letter and read the invitation from Uncle Phil and Aunt Betty, in which the two girls were asked to visit for a little while before the college was to open.

Louise continued to read, " 'We would like to solve this old mystery before most of the students arrive. A few of them are already here and you'll enjoy working with them on our campus hunt.' "

Ken interrupted, "What's the mystery?"

"The letter doesn't say," Louise replied, "but it has something to do with bringing a lot of needed money to the college."

"How do the Vikings fit in?" Chris asked.

"Uncle Phil doesn't explain, but there's supposed to be a connection." As the boys stood up to leave, she added, "I promise to have the answer the next time we see you!"

Louise and Jean accompanied the boys to their car, then returned to the living room. Presently the two relatives with whom the girls lived, walked in. One was tall, broad-shouldered Uncle Ned Dana, the other his smaller, lovely-looking sister, Aunt Harriet. Louise handed them the letter and asked if they had any new ideas about the mystery. Both shook their heads.

Uncle Ned chuckled and said, "I'm glad me hearties are puzzled. This sounds like a good mystery for you to work on. You know the old stories of the Vikings have always fascinated me, perhaps because since childhood I've loved the sea. My ship, the *Balaska*, is my second home."

"Tell us something about the Vikings," Louise requested.

Captain Dana said that these tall, muscular, red-haired warriors, natives of Scandinavian countries, had managed to take their ships to nearly every part of the world. The men plundered and murdered in order to get treasures from the natives. Around the year 1000 they reached the shores of North America.

"The Vikings apparently moved from place to place on our continent. Relics have been found in states as far apart as Minnesota and Rhode Island. Archeologists are very excited when they come across new artifacts and even pieces of the old Viking ships," Uncle Ned told the girls. "You recall their shape?" he went on. "A ship was low in the center with a row of oars on each side for sailors to use. Each end of the ship was high and usually had the figurehead of a serpent or something similar. There was one large sail, which was often striped."

As Captain Dana finished speaking, there was a loud knock on the front door. He strode to it and opened the door wide. Two large, rough-looking men hurried inside, slammed the door, and attacked Uncle Ned! One, with a mean-looking scar on his left cheek, punched and slapped him; the other, who had tight curly black hair, kicked the captain's ankles viciously.

"That'll teach you to fire me without vacation pay," the latter shouted. "And if you try to get the cops after me, you'll be in trouble. This is only a warning. Lay off or you'll get hurt bad!"

Aunt Harriet and the two girls had jumped up, amazed by the intruder's actions. They went at once to help the captain.

"Stop that!" Aunt Harriet cried out.

The two burly men paid no attention. Captain Dana was doing his best to ward off the attack, but it was difficult against two opponents.

"Come on!" Jean exclaimed to her sister.

The girls went up behind the attackers, and yanked the men's arms back. The men merely shoved the girls aside and pounced on the captain again.

Two rough-looking men attacked Uncle Ned!

"I'll call the police!" Aunt Harriet cried. She dashed to the hall telephone and began to dial a number.

"Lady, you leave that alone!" the curly-haired man yelled at her. "If you don't you'll all get hurt!"

At this moment Uncle Ned pulled himself away from his two attackers. An instant later his nieces wedged themselves between him and the strangers. Each time the intruders sidestepped to grab Captain Dana, Louise and Jean would jump in front of them. The burly men pushed the girls aside, but the tactic seemed to confuse them.

By this time Aunt Harriet had managed to contact the police. When the men heard her talking to the authorities, the one with the scar suddenly panicked. He opened the front door, shouting, "Let's get out of here!"

The two men fled down the walk. Quickly they jumped into a waiting car and sped off. The Danas tried to get the license number but from the angle where they were standing, they could not see it.

Louise asked, "Did you get a good look at the man at the wheel?"

Aunt Harriet and Jean shook their heads.

Jean remarked, "He wore a coat with a high turned-up collar. It hid most of his face."

The Danas went to sit down in living-room chairs to rest from their ordeal and to see how badly Uncle Ned was hurt. He declared he was all right, just shaken up a bit.

"It'd take more than a couple of two-bit ruffians to shake the pepper out of this old salt!" He laughed.

Louise and Jean said they felt okay, too. "None the worse for a little scrap," Jean said with a half grin.

When the police arrived, Uncle Ned suggested that the officers try to find the attackers' car, and he gave them a sketchy description of the vehicle and its passengers.

"They're two sailors from the *Balaska*," he explained. "One became very unruly and caused a lot of trouble. When he got into a fight with another crewman and injured the fellow, I discharged him. Under the circumstances he was not entitled to vacation pay. I suppose that made him mad. The other fellow is his friend, and he quit when I let the first guy go."

The policemen hurried away and drove down the street. In about fifteen minutes they returned and reported that the men and the car were not in the vicinity. "But headquarters has sent out a general alarm," one officer added.

Uncle Ned thanked them and they left. Once again the Danas sat down together to discuss the incident.

Finally the captain said, "I'd better get back to

New York to my ship before something happens there."

After a short pause he added, "I think it would be safer for you three to leave the house for a while, too. Harriet, why don't you visit one of your nearby friends? And, girls, you should start at once for your Uncle Kenmore's home at Beacon College."

Louise and Jean were delighted by their uncle's suggestion and said they would call the couple to tell them they were coming a little sooner than expected.

While Louise was making the call, Jean said to Uncle Ned, "What are the names of the two sailors who were here?"

"The shorter one with the scar on his cheek is Hoppy Canfield. The other fellow, the one I had to fire, is Lem Morehead. As you no doubt noticed, his hair is very curly, and he's tall and stocky."

Uncle Ned suggested that Aunt Harriet and the girls pack their suitcases. His sister asked, "What about lunch? I can prepare one quickly."

"All right," he said. "In the meantime, I'll call the airport and find out about plane schedules."

Captain Dana learned that he could get a flight to New York soon and one for the girls half an hour later. This would land near Still Harbor, where Beacon College was located. They would take a short flight by helicopter for the last thirty miles.

Aunt Harriet and her nieces quickly prepared sandwiches, and each took a plateful and a glass of milk upstairs, so they could eat while packing. In record time the four Danas were ready to leave the house.

Uncle Ned brought the family car from the garage, and the baggage was hastily put in the trunk. Aunt Harriet and the girls took their seats, and he drove off. All of them looked around the area to see if they could spot either of the crewmen or anyone else spying on the house. Nobody was in sight.

"I trust we've seen the last of those two horrible men," Aunt Harriet remarked.

Louise added, "Uncle Ned, I certainly hope you won't have any more trouble with them."

The captain chuckled. "I've had enough of their punches to last me for a while!"

When they reached the airport, Uncle Ned and the girls kissed Aunt Harriet good-by and hurried into the passenger terminal. They obtained their tickets, checked their bags, and a few minutes later Louise and Jean said good-by to their uncle and went off.

Just after Louise and Jean had walked through the gate, Louise glanced back, then turned and stopped short.

"What's the matter?" Jean asked. "Is something wrong?"

"I'm not sure, but I think I saw Hoppy Canfield and Lem Morehead turn the corner over there," Louise replied.

"You're kidding! What would they be doing here?"

"I have no idea, and I'm sure if we went back there we wouldn't see them. By now they've probably disappeared."

Both girls felt uneasy as they walked on. Had the two sailors followed them to the airport? And why? Neither could figure it out.

When the Danas were airborne, they began to discuss the hundred-year mystery, but did not get far. "We'll have to wait until we get there," Louise concluded.

After their plane landed at Kliegel Airport, the girls changed to a small four-passenger helicopter. The pilot, a friend of Uncle Phil Kenmore's, lived in Still Harbor, and gave the traffic reports for the local radio station. He had offered to fly the girls in on his way home in order to save them the long drive from the airport.

A likeable young man, he pointed out the sights below as they went along. "I'll come into Still Harbor across the water. Then you can see the college buildings and campus below you."

As they approached the area, the pilot began to

talk about the harbor. "Most of the time it's calm, but once in a while it kicks up a storm. There is a legend that a Viking ship broke up on the rocks here."

Suddenly the helicopter started to weave from side to side. Its pilot looked worried. He asked abruptly, "Can you girls swim?"

"Yes," Louise replied. "Why do you ask?"

"Because I'm afraid we may have to make a sudden landing in deep water!"

CHAPTER II

A Missing Codicil

LOUISE and Jean expected the helicopter to slam onto the water, perhaps losing its rotors and sinking. They hoped the terrific jolt would not knock them unconscious, so they could not swim. But if they did manage to swim to shore, what about their baggage? Would all their clothes and jewelry sink to the bottom of the harbor?

The Danas had been in many predicaments, ranging from those in *The Stone Tiger* to *The Curious Coronation*, but they had rarely been in more danger than they were in that minute. Although the blades of the copter were still turning, they were slowing down perceptibly.

Then suddenly they began to roar faster and the craft lifted into the air again.

The pilot smiled broadly. "Looks like we're home free," he said. "Relax!"

The girls breathed sighs of relief. "What was wrong with the chopper?" Jean asked.

"I don't know, except that the pressure dropped for a while. Now it's back to normal. I think we'll make it because we have only a few more minutes to go. When we arrive at the airport I'll have to check the engine thoroughly."

Louise and Jean tried to share the pilot's optimism, but they did not feel safe until the helicopter had set down at the small airfield outside Still Harbor.

The girls' Uncle Phil and Aunt Betty Kenmore, who were waiting, were happy to see their nieces. After Dr. Kenmore had greeted the pilot, the Danas thanked him for bringing them in safely, then went to their relatives' car.

"I'm so glad you could come," said Aunt Betty, smiling. She was a tall, slender blond, who taught English at the college.

Jean chuckled. "We got here about as fast as anyone possibly could after your invitation came."

Louise told her aunt and uncle what had sent them from home in such a hurry. "We don't usually run away from villains," she said. "Instead we try to capture them!"

Dr. Kenmore smiled. "Now you can put those scoundrels out of your mind and concentrate on the mystery here. The college opens in two weeks and we'll start then to get ready for our centennial celebration. We're trying very hard to locate a large sum of money, or at least a very valuable treasure, before our centennial officially begins." He added wistfully, "Beacon College is rather low on funds right now. We had a drive for pledges last spring, but it did not come up to our expectations."

"That's too bad," Louise said. "Please tell us why you can't find the treasure."

Uncle Phil promised to do so as soon as they reached home and could sit down in comfortable chairs.

"When I'm driving," he said, "I try to pay strict attention to the road. The story I'm going to tell you is too interesting and too important to be passed over lightly."

Twenty minutes later he came to the main gate of the campus, a large, wrought-iron structure, which was ornate and imposing. They entered the grounds and rode past several buildings.

Aunt Betty spoke up. "Note the unusual design on all the old structures."

Louise and Jean noticed that there were curlicue designs on all of them. The buildings themselves looked old-fashioned.

"Who founded the college?" Jean asked.

"John Beacon. It's named after him."

A few minutes later Uncle Phil pulled up in front of a large, old-fashioned wooden house,

which was well weathered. It, too, had the same, strange-looking design running across the upper part of the large porch.

"This was the original Beacon homestead," Aunt Betty explained. "It's about two hundred years old."

She and the girls got out of the car and went up the porch steps. The Danas were amazed at how well everything had been preserved, and concluded that the house must have been marvelously built.

The interior was roomy and high ceilinged. It had a center hall flanked by a large room on each side.

When Jean mentioned this fact, Aunt Betty said, "Wait until you see your bedroom! You'll almost get lost in it!" Then she added, "This house used to be the general administration building, but when college attendance increased, the trustees had a larger, more modern building constructed. The various presidents of Beacon have lived here ever since."

She led the way upstairs to show the girls their bedroom. As she had said, it was enormous. Jean giggled. "We could have a dance up here!"

There was a fireplace in the room. The mantel was decorated with the same design as the one on the outside of the house.

"The Beacons must have loved this pattern, which makes me curious," Louise said. "I'd like to look at it more closely to see if it has any significance."

Later, after everyone had returned to the living room, Dr. Kenmore began his story of the hundred-year mystery. He said that John Beacon's will had mentioned a codicil he intended to add to it. No one was to open the sealed codicil for one hundred years. On the centennial anniversary of the college, directions for finding a treasure that would greatly benefit the college would be revealed in the codicil.

"Fortunately, the Beacons had a very fine firm of lawyers, whose successors are still practicing today. They carried out all the instructions of the will."

Louise asked eagerly, "Even to the point of not opening the codicil until one hundred years later?"

Dr. Kenmore nodded. "That's the catch," he said. "It is believed that John Beacon, founder of the college, died before he could deliver the codicil. In fact, our lawyers are not even sure he completed it. They do know, however, that there was a treasure, that Beacon wanted the college to have it on its centennial celebration, and that the codicil or some other clue to the treasure's whereabouts may be somewhere on campus."

"How strange!" Jean said. "No one has any idea what's in the codicil?"

"No," her uncle replied.

He went on to say that John Beacon was a bachelor. He had no family left and therefore no relative to whom to leave his estate, which was large. He had willed his property to the coed college and left enough money to finance it for at least a hundred years.

"He must have been psychic, because now, at our centennial celebration, the college exchequer is low. One theory is that Mr. Beacon, for some reason, decided to hide the codicil, and that when money was running low, an extra effort would be made to find the codicil and get the directions to the treasure."

Uncle Phil told the girls that a new search team had been formed of students, who had been asked to come back early and try to find the codicil before the opening of college.

Louise and Jean looked at each other. Then Louise said to Dr. Kenmore, "You are paying us a great compliment, inviting us to join your search team. When will we meet the others?"

The college president smiled. "Oh, you'll meet them, but they're divided into pairs. Each couple is looking separately, so we can be sure that every spot on or near the campus will be thoroughly investigated. We feel that the lawyers have done everything else."

When Dr. Kenmore paused, Aunt Betty spoke up. "My husband hasn't told you that the will says the codicil contains a great secret handed down through generations of the Beacon family and never told to anyone else, which will bring a priceless inheritance to the college."

At this moment the front doorbell rang, and Aunt Betty went to answer it. She let in an attractive young couple, who, she said, would be seniors this year.

"Let me introduce Debra Hood and Paul Kraft. Deb and Paul, these are Louise and Jean Dana, our nieces, who have come to join your search team. They are skillful amateur detectives."

The four young people shook hands and the Danas said they were delighted to meet the couple who were part of the search team. Deb and Paul, in turn, remarked that they were excited about working with the Dana detectives.

Deb added, "I'm sure you girls can teach us a lot, so we may be pestering you!"

Jean's eyes twinkled. "If you bother us, we'll give you some clues and put you to work!"

Everyone laughed, then Paul asked if Louise and Jean would like to take a ride around the campus. "We'll give you a personally conducted tour."

"How about it?" Louise asked the Kenmores.

Aunt Betty replied, "Go ahead. There's plenty of time before dinner will be ready. I'd like you young folks to get better acquainted."

The four went off. During the ride Deb and Paul pointed out new buildings and old ones.

Paul remarked, "Did Dr. Kenmore tell you that when the treasure is found, he hopes to use part of it to add a new course to the archeology department?"

"No," Louise answered.

"This one will be strictly for the study of Vikings," Paul said. "Their history in Europe, their arrival on our shores, and their hieroglyphics, which were carved on many rune stones that are being found in this country."

"Uncle Phil didn't mention any of that," Louise replied, "but it sounds very exciting. I'd like to take the course myself!"

Presently Paul parked his car and suggested that they walk to the cliff. "There's an interesting gazebo there," he said.

Louise and Jean puckered their brows, trying to remember what a gazebo was. Deb saw the expression on their faces and said, "You know, a gazebo is an open summerhouse that is tall and wide. Its domed roof is supported by round pillars and it has no floor."

"I'm glad you explained," Jean told her.

Before they reached the edge of the cliff, they came upon the handsome structure. The Danas had seen pictures of similar ones in foreign countries.

"I want to show you something interesting inside the gazebo," Deb remarked.

She led the way to the spacious waterfront building and pointed to a large tapered stone standing upright in the center. It was embedded in the ground.

Louise asked, "Isn't this a stela?"

"Yes," Deb replied, "and look at the design on it. The strange markings go all the way around."

The Danas noticed that a short distance below the top of the stela was the same design that had now become familiar to them.

Paul spoke up. "Those are supposed to be Viking characters, but experts who have come here to read symbols have had no luck. If it has any meaning, nobody knows what it is."

As the young people walked outside, Louise remarked, "This place is full of mysteries!"

Deb said, "An atmosphere of mystery sort of goes with the territory." She pointed to the cliff. "Ever since I heard the story of the Viking ship being blown in here and broken up during a violent storm, I've had a lot of respect for this harbor."

The young people walked as close as they dared to the edge and looked down into the water. Below its surface they could see sharp, jagged rocks.

"No wonder the ship was wrecked!" Louise said.

"It gets really rough down there when the tide comes in," Deb said, "and during a storm it's frightening."

"Has anyone ever fallen off the cliff?" Louise inquired.

"No," Paul replied, "but this area has been declared off limits after dark. Dr. Kenmore says it's too dangerous and won't allow any students here at night."

He had just finished speaking when the rock on which Jean had been standing suddenly began to wobble precariously. She spread her arms out in an attempt to regain her balance.

"Oh!" Deb screamed.

CHAPTER III

Viking Ships

As Jean fought desperately to avoid falling down the cliff, Louise, who was nearest her, sprang forward and grabbed her arm. She pulled her up to level ground, and the two girls sat down.

"Wow!" Jean exclaimed.

Louise was speechless. Through her mind had rushed visions of what could have happened to Jean if she had tumbled down the steep, rocky embankment!

Paul walked over to the rock. He dropped down on his knees and examined the spot where the large stone lay.

"Someone has tampered with this!" he called back. "All the dirt around the rock has been loosened. Jean, you're lucky!"

"I guess I am," she replied. "And also a little dumb. I should have tested the rock before stepping on it with both feet!"

The others agreed, but were thankful she had not been hurt. Paul came back and sat down on the grass with the girls.

Louise asked, "Who would have done such a thing and why?"

Deb thought it could have been a student searcher who thought the missing codicil might have been buried beneath the rock.

Paul disagreed. "They're too well trained to have left anything that dangerous for someone to step on!"

Jean remarked that while she and Louise had made many enemies since they had begun solving mysteries, she doubted that any of them knew the girls were here at Beacon College.

"So I'd rule out any of those people."

Louise thought so, too. "I have nothing to offer by way of a solution, but I predict that sooner or later we'll find out."

"It's just possible," Paul said, "that there's some sadistic person around here who enjoys watching people get hurt."

At this remark the four searchers rose from the grass and began to look around for anyone who might be spying on them. They could see no one.

Louise said, "Jean, I think you and I should return at once to the Kenmore house and report the incident. I'm sure Uncle Phil will want to do something about it."

They said good-by to Paul and Deb and hurried

away. As they expected, their relatives were upset.

At once Dr. Kenmore said, "I shall have a sturdy fence erected at the steepest part of that cliff!"

"I suppose," said Louise, "that you will put it up in such a hurry there won't be time to paint a design on it."

"That's right," her uncle replied. He added, however, that probably decorations would be needed to make the fence match the other campus structures. "We'll do that later."

"Would you use the same Viking design as the one on the buildings?" Louise asked him.

Uncle Phil smiled. "That's an idea. I suppose everything here should be consistent. But such work will take time. Right now the fence must be put up, even if it's temporary."

He also said he would issue an order for the rock to be removed entirely or sunk deeper into the cliff.

Aunt Betty told the girls she was a little nervous, thinking about a malicious person sneaking around the campus. Her husband tried to assure her that a guard patrolled the area very often and would detect anything suspicious.

Louise and Jean made no comment, but felt that the guard had not done a good job as far as the rock was concerned. And up to now they had not seen him anywhere. Jean mentioned this and her uncle said the man had been ill and no one had been appointed to replace him. "I'll attend to it."

The following morning, before Dr. Kenmore went to his office, he asked the Danas what work they were going to undertake that day. "Will you begin your search?"

Louise replied, "I'm intrigued by the design on this house and the other buildings. Maybe it has some significance. In any case, I'm going to study it."

She got a notebook and pencil and copied the pattern, which repeated itself every few feet, or inches, depending on the size of the object on which it had been carved. The ends of each section had arced saucer-shaped designs with decorative ends. Between them were vertical and horizontal strips.

Louise measured each item and found that the designs were exact replicas and had been scaled down or up in proportion to the area on which they appeared. There were no open spaces in the design.

Louise decided to concentrate on the drawing. She examined it with a magnifying glass, but saw nothing to indicate that the design meant anything.

She carried the drawing to the college library and compared it with other Viking designs. Then she studied a number of books on Viking history. Still she found nothing conclusive. Finally the young sleuth went back to the Kenmores' and inspected the design on the house again.

Suddenly an idea came to her. She rushed inside to show the drawing to Aunt Betty. Jean had already left the house.

"You know what I think these saucerlike figures on the ends of the design are supposed to be?" Louise asked. "I believe they're meant to be Viking ships!"

Mrs. Kenmore looked at Louise's sketch. "You know, I think you're right. I've lived here for four years and never noticed this!" She added, "What significance do you think the ships have?"

Louise shrugged. "Right now I haven't the faintest idea. But since the original settlers whose ship was wrecked in the harbor were Vikings, this design might have been a copy of their vessel."

Aunt Betty smiled. "That's an interesting thought. Will you pursue it?"

"Indeed I will," her niece replied. "And I think it would be a good idea to let the rest of the search team know about my theory. Maybe someone in the group has a suggestion."

Both Dr. Kenmore and Jean were amazed at Louise's findings. The college president said he would call a meeting of the entire search group that afternoon so they could discuss it.

Five couples arrived and were enthusiastic about Louise's idea. A boy named Dick Mason spoke up. "If this means the missing codicil is hidden in a Viking ship, I know where we may find it."

"Where?" the others asked.

Dick said there was a large model of a Viking ship on display in the library.

"Let's go right over there and examine it," Jean suggested.

The group hurried across the campus into one of the newer buildings. The Danas noticed that while the architecture was compatible with the old buildings, it was definitely more modern. No design had been put on the structure, but a space about three feet high across the front, just under the roof line had been left blank. They assumed that some day the library would be decorated with Viking ships and horizontal and vertical lines.

When the search team entered the building, the head librarian, Miss Wiley, greeted them. Louise introduced the group, then explained why they had come.

The librarian smiled. "That old Viking ship has suddenly become popular. Two men were here yesterday, examining it thoroughly."

"People from the college?" Louise asked.

Miss Wiley shook her head. "No. They said they were professors from another college."

The Danas were suspicious. "What did these men look like?" she asked.

"They were both dark, but one had straight hair, the other very curly hair. The fellow with the straight hair had a mean scar on his left cheek."

As Louise and Jean listened, their eyes met. Could the visitors, by some chance have been the sailors from the *Balaska* who had attacked Uncle Ned? The descriptions sounded as if they could have been Hoppy Canfield and Lem Morehead!

At this point Deb asked the Danas, "You have such funny expressions on your faces. Do you know the men?"

Louise admitted that perhaps they did. She asked Miss Wiley, "Did those professors ask any questions or make any comments about the college or anyone here?"

The answer was no. "They studied the Viking ship thoroughly, then left," the librarian said.

The search team examined the old Viking ship model, and Paul remarked, "Louise, I see now where you got your idea that the saucerlike design represents a Viking ship. This one has a high bow and stern."

Miss Wiley watched in fascination as Louise and Jean opened every compartment of the ship model, tapped it, then finally set it back on the shelf.

"I'm sure it doesn't contain anything of importance," Jean remarked.

The others in their group agreed, thanked Miss Wiley, and left. The Danas returned to the Kenmore house and told Aunt Betty about the two strangers who had gone to the library.

"We wonder if they could have been the two crew members from the *Balaska* who attacked Uncle Ned," Louise remarked.

"Oh, I hope not!" their aunt exclaimed. "I don't want any harm to come to you while you're here."

Jean suggested that they get in touch with Uncle Phil and ask him to notify the police about the suspects. She phoned him, and he promised to take care of the matter immediately.

"I'll be home soon," he added. "I hope your Aunt Betty has a good dinner waiting."

As soon as Dr. Kenmore returned, he began opening mail addressed to him at the house. Holding up one envelope, he remarked to Aunt Betty and the girls, "This is a strange-looking letter."

The address on the envelope was printed and there was no return address. The postmark was Pleasant View, which Uncle Phil said was a seashore resort not far from Still Harbor.

He slipped his thumb under the flap and tore the letter open. After he had perused the contents, he read aloud:

I HAVE THE MISSING BEACON CODICIL. IT CAME INTO MY HANDS BY MISTAKE. I WILL SELL IT TO THE COLLEGE FOR $100,000. I ASSURE YOU THE CONTENTS ARE WORTH A LOT MORE THAN THAT. SEND YOUR REPLY TO WILLIAM KARPA-LOW, GENERAL DELIVERY.

His listeners were stunned for a moment, then Aunt Betty burst out, "That's a holdup! The trustees of the college would never vote to send money, especially so much, to an extortionist!"

Dr. Kenmore's mouth had set into a straight line. "You are absolutely right."

Louise and Jean stared at the professor. Finally Louise asked, "What will you do about the letter, Uncle Phil?"

CHAPTER IV

The Ghost

Uncle Phil Kenmore decided to ignore the demand of a hundred thousand dollars. Louise and Jean looked at each other. They both felt that this was not the way to catch the extortionist.

Finally Louise spoke. "You asked us to come here to help you solve the mystery," she said. "May I suggest that you send a phony reply to Mr. Karpalow and have the police set up a stakeout to seize him at the post office?"

Jean added, "Why don't you let Louise and me go? Mr. Karpalow doesn't know us and we could act like any other summer visitors stopping in at the post office."

Dr. Kenmore looked at his wife. "What do you think of that idea?" he asked.

"It's a very good one," Aunt Betty answered.

Her husband smiled and gave in. "But there's one condition," he said. "I want the police to capture Mr. Karpalow or anyone he may send to get the note. You girls are not to take any risks—you're too precious to me and your aunt. We wouldn't want you to get hurt."

The Danas laughed and promised. Uncle Phil wrote the note at once and sent it. "I'm sure it will get there by tomorrow," he said. "Take my car in the morning and try to track down Karpalow."

The two young detectives could hardly wait for the next day to come. They felt sure that whether or not Mr. Karpalow was caught, he knew something about the codicil and they might pick up a good clue.

When they reached the Pleasant View post office the following day, Louise inquired if Mr. Karpalow had been there or if he had sent anyone for his mail.

"I don't know," said the young woman in charge. "Just a minute." A card in the window read *Miss Mary Dole*.

She disappeared for several seconds, then came back to say the man had rented a box. It was now empty.

"Has the morning mail come in yet?" Louise asked her.

"No," Miss Dole replied.

"When will it be here?"

The young woman looked at the clock. "In about half an hour."

"We'll be back," Jean said. "Come on, Louise, let's look around town a bit."

Before leaving, Louise thought she would tell the clerk why she and her sister were so inquisitive. She smiled and winked one eye.

"We think he's a person we've been trying to contact," she said, "and that he's using an assumed name."

"I understand," said Miss Dole and winked back.

Within half an hour the Danas returned. A mail truck had just delivered letters and packages, and they were now being sorted.

The postal clerk noticed the girls. Through the little window she whispered, "The box you want to watch is number fifteen."

"Thanks," said Louise, smiling.

Dr. Kenmore's letter had arrived and was put into Mr. Karpalow's box. The girls stood around a while, then went over to a desk and began to address postcards they had purchased in town. They finished their chore, but Mr. Karpalow had not come in.

Jean said to Louise, "We can't hang around here all day. I'm getting hungry and my feet hurt!"

"Let's give the man until noon," Louise suggested. "Then we'll go outside."

Twelve o'clock came, and in disappointment

the Danas walked to the door. They paused a moment to speak to Miss Dole.

"We're going out for a little while. We understand the police have a stakeout here, so if Mr. Karpalow comes in, he'll be caught."

"Police?" Miss Dole asked, startled. "You didn't say anything about the police!"

"No, we didn't," Louise replied. "But Mr. Karpalow is wanted by them."

Before Miss Dole could ask any more questions, Louise and Jean hurried away. As they walked out of the post office, both stopped in their tracks. Two men were watching them from across the street.

Excited, Jean exclaimed, "Those are Uncle Ned's attackers!"

Apparently the men recognized the Danas at the same moment and began to run down the street at a fast clip. The girls pursued them. In a moment, Hoppy and Lem turned a corner.

When the girls reached it, Lem was yelling at a third man standing by a car. "Start the engine!" As soon as he and Hoppy got to the car, it took off and sped down the street.

In disgust, Louise and Jean gave up the chase. Though it looked old and was dirty green, the car had plenty of power. The girls knew that by the time they ran back to their own car, the men would be well out of sight.

"Do you suppose Hoppy and Lem know Karpalow?" Jean asked her sister.

"I'll bet they do," Louise replied, "and they were waiting for a chance to get into the post office without being observed."

"This complicates matters," Jean remarked.

"Maybe not," Louise replied. "Knowing Hoppy and Lem are here might make it easier for us to locate the villain who's trying to extort a hundred thousand dollars from Beacon College."

On their way back to the car the girls passed police headquarters and went inside. They reported the incident to the sergeant in charge, who said he would pass the word along to the chief.

"We'll keep the post office under observation for a few days and alert all the postal workers to the man we're looking for. If he shows up, we'll nab him and call you."

After a quick lunch, Louise and Jean rode back to the Kenmores'.

"What happened?" Aunt Betty greeted them.

Jean answered, "I guess you'd call it a plus and a minus." She described the incident, and added, "I wonder if Mr. Karpalow realizes he's being watched and whether he plans to pick up Uncle Phil's letter."

"In case he doesn't, how will he know what the contents are?" Aunt Betty asked.

"If he senses we have the police after him,"

Louise replied, "he'll realize the letter is probably a setup. I'll call the post office and find out if there is any news."

She went to the telephone and spoke with Miss Dole. Louise learned some startling news. The letter in Box 15 had been removed, but no one seemed to know when, how, or by whom. Since the police lookout was still stationed there, watching the entrance, it was assumed that the man who took the letter had sneaked in through the employees' entrance at the rear and had somehow picked it up.

When Aunt Betty heard this, she said, "What a pity! I guess somebody wasn't on the job! How could it possibly have happened?"

Jean suggested that if the person who picked up the letter had disguised himself as one of the postal workers, he could have pulled off his little scheme easily.

The Danas were annoyed and felt that their brainstorm had come to nothing. Jean said she was going outside to walk around the campus to get a new inspiration.

Louise decided to stay indoors and work further on the mysterious design that appeared in so many places. After staring at the pattern for an hour she decided that it looked like a jumble of curved and straight pieces. She went to the kitchen, helped herself to a glass of milk, and walked around the garden.

Soon she wanted to continue her work. She went back to the sheets on which she had scribbled all sorts of possibilities, which appeared to mean nothing. Louise picked up one of the papers and began to rotate it.

Suddenly the girl sleuth detected something she had not noticed before. The vertical and horizontal lines seemed to form the initials E L or L E!

Recalling the Viking interest of the Beacon family, Louise thought, "Those initials could stand for Leif Erikson! I wonder if the Beacons are descendants of that famous explorer and that's why they used his initials in making this design."

At this moment Jean returned. Louise's eyes were gleaming with excitement. "I think I have a great clue!" she said, and showed her sister the initials.

"That's amazing!" Jean exclaimed. "Now that you tell me, the L E or E L stand out very prominently. How come we didn't see the letters before?"

"It's an age-old truth—we missed the forest because of the trees!"

A little while later Uncle Phil and Aunt Betty walked into the room. When they were told the exciting news, both were thrilled with their niece's discovery.

"You girls are terrific detectives," Uncle Phil said. "I wonder what you'll discover next."

"Do you think this will bring you any closer to

finding the missing codicil?" Aunt Betty asked.

Louise shrugged. "I really don't know, but I have a feeling that this pattern will help us to solve the mystery. It's no more than a hunch, but I can't get the idea out of my mind."

After dinner Paul and Deb dropped in. When they were shown the drawing and initials, the couple was surprised and impressed. "I never would have thought of that," Deb admitted.

After some more conversation, Paul suggested that the four go out for a walk around the campus. "It's a beautiful night," he said. "We shouldn't miss it."

With no definite direction in mind, the young people found themselves heading for the gazebo. Jean turned back a couple of times, and Paul asked, "What is it? Do you think we're being followed?"

"I don't know. I thought I heard a noise, but now everything seems to be quiet."

The four stood still for a few minutes, straining their ears, but could hear nothing but the faraway chirp of crickets. They went on.

Presently the four friends came within sight of the tall, imposing summerhouse. Suddenly Deb gasped. "Look!" she whispered.

Flitting through the gazebo was a ghost!

CHAPTER V

Kidnap Scare

ACCOMPANIED by chanters, the ghost danced, gliding back and forth in the gazebo, waving its arms and twisting and turning in circles. The others uttered weird, unintelligible sounds in drawn-out sing-song voices.

Louise and Jean were neither frightened nor convinced by the weird performance. It seemed staged.

Jean said, "Probably these are college people practicing for a play."

Deb shook her head nervously. "Not at this time of year. That takes place only during the months when the college is in full session." She was frightened.

The young people continued to move forward until they were within a few yards of the gazebo.

Louise whispered to the others, "That ghost is awkward in his sheet. I'll bet it's a man!"

Jean urged that they all get much closer and expose the performers. She hurried ahead onto the floor of the gazebo.

"Come back!" Paul called out. "You know you have enemies!"

Undaunted, Jean faced the ghost and said, "Who are you, and why are you here?"

There was no answer. Jean started to speak again, but at this instant the ghost, definitely a man, swooped her up in his arms and dashed from the summerhouse toward the newly built fence.

"Oh!" Deb screamed.

With Louise and Paul she hurried after the mysterious figure. He was fleet-footed, but when he reached the end of the fence, Jean was trying so hard to break away from him that she almost made him lose his balance.

Just as he was about to start scaling down the precipice with her, Louise, Deb, and Paul caught up to them. They reached out and grabbed Jean.

In the scuffle, Paul had managed to pull the sheet from the ghost. They all hoped to identify him, but even in the dim moonlight they realized that he wore a stocking mask over his face. By now he was quickly scrambling down the face of the rocky cliff.

"Shall we follow him?" Louise asked.

Paul said definitely not, and Jean added, "That man is as strong as an ox. I wouldn't advise it."

The pursuers gave up and turned their attention

The ghost swooped Jean up in his arms!

to the chanters. But there was no sign of them, and when the searchers reached the gazebo, no one was in sight.

Louise and Jean looked across the campus. They could barely discern a few black-garmented figures hurrying off in the distance.

"Don't think you can get away with this!" Jean shouted at them.

In answer one of the figures called back, "You'd better give Mr. Karpalow the money, or worse things will happen to you!"

Jean was defiant. As they disappeared, she cried out, "We think he's a faker and we won't give him a cent!"

The four young people headed for the Kenmore home. The college president and his wife were astonished to learn that someone had attempted to kidnap Jean.

Her uncle's lips set in a grim line. "This whole thing has gone far enough! From now on we'll double our surveillance!"

"Who do you think the attacker was?" Paul asked.

Louise told him he could be any one of at least three people. They suspected the man named Karpalow and the two sailors from Uncle Ned's ship who had come to their home and fought with him. She explained why.

"Now we're pretty sure they are connected somehow with this Mr. Karpalow. Maybe they knew him before, or possibly they followed Jean and me here to harrass us, and met Karpalow."

"No matter who or what," said Uncle Phil, "I still feel that this whole thing has gone far enough. I invited you, Louise and Jean, up here to solve a baffling mystery, but I never realized there'd be any danger attached to it."

Louise looked crestfallen. "Does this mean you're going to send us home?"

"Oh, please don't do that!" Jean begged him.

The college president looked at his wife, and suddenly smiled. "No, we're not going to send you home. But I insist that from now on you be very careful. Try to stay together at all times."

Louise said, "Oh, thank you. We promise to watch out, and like all good detectives, we'll look in four directions at once. If we can't do that, then I'll look two ways, and Jean the other two."

The others laughed, and then Deb and Paul said they must leave. In a short while, Louise and Jean said good night to their uncle and aunt, and were just about to go to their room, when the phone rang.

Dr. Kenmore answered. "Hello?"

There was no answer on the other end. He was about to hang up when a man said, "Karpalow wants to make a deal. A hundred thousand dollars for the codicil. If you are willing to go along with the scheme, put an ad in the local paper. Karpalow will then contact you about when and where the exchange is to take place. He has worked out a perfect plan. Do not try to involve the police unless you want to endanger the lives of your nieces and your wife. If Karpalow doesn't see your ad soon, you'll be in trouble!"

"I won't do it!" Dr. Kenmore thundered. "Who are you?"

A click in the phone told him the caller had hung up.

"What is it, Uncle Phil?" Louise asked. "Who was calling?"

"Karpalow or one of his buddies," Dr. Kenmore replied, frowning, and he told them what the stranger had said.

"He has a lot of nerve, threatening you!" Jean said hotly. "Of course you're not going along with his demand!"

"I don't intend to," Uncle Phil said. "But you two must be especially cautious. Betty, you too. Don't go out alone, ever."

"We won't," the three assured him, and then the girls went to bed.

The following morning, while the family was at breakfast, Dr. Kenmore left the table to answer the front doorbell. With thoughts of the threats fresh in their minds, the other three followed him. To everyone's surprise no one was waiting to be admitted.

Uncle Phil looked left and right, but saw nobody. A moment later he detected a white envelope lying on the doormat. It was addressed to him. He picked it up, a puzzled look on his face.

After opening the envelope and reading the contents of the letter, he turned to the others and remarked, "Well, this is a new turn of events!"

CHAPTER VI

Attic Secret

Louise and Jean hoped their uncle would divulge the contents of the note quickly, but they did not want to ask him to do so. They looked toward Aunt Betty, hoping she would urge him. She did not fail them.

"Please don't keep us waiting, Phil," she pleaded. "We want to hear what's in the note, and why you think it's a new turn of events."

"I know this will surprise you," her husband replied. He read the note:

PAY NO ATTENTION TO KARPALOW. HE IS A LIAR AND STUPID. I KNOW WHERE THE CODICIL IS, BUT I AM TOO OLD AND TOO ILL TO HUNT FOR IT. I WANT THE COLLEGE TO HAVE IT AND WILL SEND DIRECTIONS BY MAIL.

This was, indeed, a new twist. Louise asked, "Who sent that?"

"There is no signature," her uncle replied. "It simply says, 'A former grounds keeper.'"

"That sounds reasonable," said Aunt Betty. "But why wouldn't he sign his name?"

The college president told them he did not believe the note was authentic. "There's no reason why the person shouldn't have signed it. Besides, leaving it on my doorstep makes it seem even more suspicious."

Louise said, "Uncle Phil, you mentioned that the note was a new twist. Do you think this is from Karpalow using a sly method to get the treasure?"

"Who knows?" Dr. Kenmore replied.

"Maybe one of the former grounds keepers did discover the codicil but for some reason has kept it a secret until now," Aunt Betty put in. She offered to look up the names of former grounds keepers to find out if their employment files could possibly provide a clue. "I think we have some records here that were never transferred to the new administration building."

She went to her husband's study and was gone for fifteen minutes. When she returned, Aunt Betty shook her head. "No clues there. Every grounds keeper up to the present one has died."

"Then that means," Louise said, "this note *is* a phony."

Dr. Kenmore remarked that he was disturbed by the appearance of a second message and its reverse approach. He suggested that they disregard it and that the girls start on a new angle in their search.

Louise said perhaps she would work again on the design that appeared on many buildings and the stela. Jean admitted that for the moment she was at a loss to think of a new approach to their investigation.

"I have a suggestion," Aunt Betty said. "We have a most wonderful old attic in this house. Supposedly it was thoroughly searched by Mr. Beacon's lawyers, who declared they had found nothing. However, after watching you girls work on this mystery, I'm sure you will get some new ideas if you go up there and look around."

At once Louise and Jean were eager to see the ancient attic. They followed Aunt Betty up two flights of stairs and found themselves in an immense room. It was surprisingly clean—none of the cobwebs or dust one might have expected.

"I'll leave you girls here," their aunt said. "Good luck!"

After she had gone downstairs, Louise and Jean began to examine various articles. Louise noticed an old-fashioned doll seated in a rocking chair. The whole thing was covered with cellophane.

Louise removed the covering and held up the doll. Although it had a babyish face, the body was clothed in an elaborate grown-up dress, cape, and matching bonnet. They were made of blue silk, which was now faded.

"Jean, come and see this adorable toy!" Louise called to her sister.

Jean hurried over and giggled at the many ruffled petticoats the doll was wearing. "She's perfect, except one shoe is missing." She picked up the other foot and said, "This black kid slipper has a number on the bottom. It looks like eighteen twelve."

"Maybe that's the date when the doll was made," Louise suggested.

Jean nodded, then said, "It's possible that this was a birthday gift to some little girl and the year was put on the shoe."

"Here's another guess," said Louise. "Eighteen twelve was the year of the United States Naval War. Maybe it had something to do with that."

Both girls examined the doll thoroughly. It yielded no clue to help them locate the missing codicil. Louise put the toy back in its rocking chair and covered them once more with the cellophane.

"Did you find anything interesting?" Louise asked her sister.

Jean said she had just opened a very old trunk, which was full of antique clothes and draperies. "Let's take them out and examine each one carefully."

The Danas were fascinated by the drapes because all of them were made of velvet with hand-painted designs. Jean held one up. It was maroon in color and had sprays of pink dogwood painted on it.

"How elegant!" Jean said. "Imagine having that hanging at a window. It would be like another painting on the wall."

By this time Louise had pulled one of the dresses from the trunk. "I think I'll try this on," she said. "It's made of silk and sounds nice when it rustles." She slipped the dark-blue fitted garment over her head, then ran her arms into the sleeves. "Jean, please fasten the back."

When her sister saw it, she exclaimed, "There must be a hundred hooks and eyes on here!" After a short pause, she burst into laughter.

"What's so funny?" Louise asked.

"My dear Cinderella, how you have grown!" Jean said. "Louise, this dress won't come within three inches of going around you!"

Louise was astounded. "And to think I only wear size eight!"

She suggested that Jean try to get into one of the elaborate creations. Her sister tried to put on a white lace wedding dress. It would not fit by at least four inches!

"This must be a size four," she said. "Oh, well, I understand that the whole human race is gradually growing larger. Since revolutionary times, girls have become taller and more muscular."

Jean giggled again. "And I understand our hands and feet are much longer."

The girls now made a painstaking examination of everything in the trunk, including the hems of the dresses, where papers might have been concealed, but found neither the missing codicil nor any clue to its location.

Near the trunk stood a long, narrow box. Louise opened it and Jean lifted out a carefully wrapped object. It proved to be a miniature model of a Viking ship. Every detail, including the oars, was beautifully carved. There was no date on it, but Jean spotted four almost obliterated letters, which spelled THOR.

"Thor," Louise repeated. "He was the old Norse god of thunder."

The girls looked at every outside inch of the Viking vessel, but could find no clues to the ship's origin.

"Do you suppose," Jean said, "that this ship could be a model of the one that was smashed to pieces in Still Harbor?"

"Could be," Louise agreed. "Maybe we've found the hiding place of the codicil, or at least directions to it."

The girls carried the ship model to a window so that they could examine the inside of the cabin minutely. They could barely detect what must be a footlocker and managed to slide a small door aside. In the enclosed area lay a stone. Louise reached in and pulled it out.

Jean held the object up to the light. "It has a

picture on it and symbols. It must be a rune stone!"

The girls could decipher nothing from the picture and symbols. Both of them were so excited by their find, however, that they decided to go downstairs and ask the Kenmores if they had ever seen the stone and whether they understood its message.

The college president was just returning from his office. He saw the girls' faces flushed with excitement. "Now what are you young ladies up to?" he asked.

Louise opened her palm. "Have you ever seen this before?"

Her uncle picked up the rune stone and turned it over and over. "No, I never have, and it looks most interesting. Where did you find it?"

The girls told him. Then the three went to find Aunt Betty. She had never seen the ancient stone either. She admitted having seen the model of the Viking ship many times, and had shown it to visitors, but had never examined the interior.

"I think," said Dr. Kenmore, "that I should take this immediately to my friend Professor Halsey. He is an authority on old Norse symbols." He turned to his nieces. "Would you like to come along?"

"Oh, yes!" both girls replied.

They set off in Dr. Kenmore's car. He thought that Professor Halsey might be in his laboratory and drove there. Fortunately, the elderly gentle-man was in. He was a kindly-looking, gray-haired man who wore heavy spectacles.

Dr. Kenmore handed him the rune stone and said, "Bob, what do you make of this?"

The professor studied it for several seconds, then said excitedly, "This is amazing! What a wonderful find! Where did you get it?"

CHAPTER VII

The Ancient Cellar

PROFESSOR Halsey led the way from the laboratory to his private office. Here there were shelves and shelves of books. He explained to the girls that most of them were his private collection on the Vikings, the Scandinavian countries, and emigrations to other countries of the world.

"They were hardy seamen all right," he remarked, and smiled. "I'm sure the oceans weren't any calmer then than they are now. How those sailors managed to get so far in their long boats never fails to astonish me."

He pointed to two shelves. "I've written these books based on my own adventures," he explained. "I'd appreciate it if you would tell me exactly where you found this rune stone."

After hearing the story, he turned to another section of his books and finally pulled one out.

"Now I'll see if I can translate the message on this," he said.

The Dana girls and their uncle sat quietly, waiting. The professor alternately smiled and frowned. Was he amused or puzzled? Jean began to grow fidgety, and finally stood up. She crossed the room to the bookshelf on which magazines were kept. After she had looked at some interesting pictures of ancient wrecks, she was interrupted by Professor Halsey.

"Sorry to have taken so long," he said, "but after I first translated the message, I couldn't believe I was right, so I worked on the symbols some more."

"What was your first translation?" Jean asked, curious.

The professor began to laugh. He threw the rune stone into the air, then caught it again and laughed even harder.

Dr. Kenmore and the girls looked at one another questioningly. "Won't you let us in on the joke?" Louise urged.

"I thought it said, 'The fish who swallows me will have a stomachache!' "

Now the others broke out in gay laughter too.

"Maybe the Viking who engraved this had a sense of humor," Jean suggested.

Professor Halsey shook his head. "No, I don't think that was the correct translation. After working on it some more, I came up with another meaning. And this one is anything but funny. In fact, it's rather sinister."

"Let's hear it," Jean urged.

" 'He who rides in this ship will sink.' "

"It is a warning," Louise said thoughtfully. "And a rather scary one."

"I wonder what it means," Jean said.

"Well, it's obvious, isn't it?" Louise stated. "The stone was put on a doomed ship."

"But the ship model is still around, after all these years!" Jean objected.

Dr. Kenmore chuckled. "That's because no one ever sailed in it to sink the model."

Professor Halsey turned to Dr. Kenmore. "Phil, I'd like to keep this rune stone if you don't mind. I want to use it in one of my classes. Maybe a student will come up with another translation."

The callers said good-by, thanking the man for his help, and went back to the Kenmore house. Louise and Jean returned to the attic, wrapped the ship model carefully, and put it back in its chest.

Their search went on for some time among wardrobes, boxes, and old newspapers. They found no clues to help them in their hunt for the missing codicil. After making sure there was nothing more in the old attic they went back downstairs.

The two girls were preparing for bed that evening when Jean said, "Well, what next?"

Louise reminded her that the only place in the house they had not examined was the cellar.

"These old houses usually have very interesting basements," she remarked. "Why don't we go down there right after breakfast tomorrow?"

They mentioned this to Aunt Betty and Uncle Phil, who thought it would be a good idea.

"You'll find it somewhat different from the general run of old cellars," Aunt Betty said. "This one is really a series of zigzagging corridors with rooms opening off them."

The next morning Uncle Phil led his nieces to the cellar door, which opened from the kitchen. Hanging on the wall leading downstairs were two strong lantern searchlights. He told the girls to take them.

When Louise and Jean reached the foot of the steps, they found that the area had been completely cleaned out. Evidently it was no longer used for storage.

The overhead light did not cast its beam beyond the immediate area that led into a narrow corridor. Louise and Jean turned on their searchlights and started to walk along the earthen floor.

The place was damp and musty. Presently they came to a door and opened it. Their lights revealed nothing but an old cot. They flashed the lights all over the ceiling and walls but detected nothing.

Louise closed the door, and they proceeded along the corridor. A few seconds later the searchers came to another room. After examining it carefully, they decided nothing was hidden in the ceiling or walls. On the floor stood two empty jugs. Each girl turned one upside down, but no hidden object fell out. They set the jugs back and went on.

Suddenly Louise stopped. "Which way are we going?" she asked.

"I'd say north," Jean replied. "Why?"

Louise said she thought if this was true, and it probably was, then the corridor was not under the house. It extended beyond the building.

"It's like a secret passageway," Jean said. "I wonder where it goes."

The rocky tunnel suddenly turned a sharp corner. From this point on the walls looked quite different. The stones that formed the ceiling and sides were not piled up as one would expect to find underground, but had been placed in a definite zigzag pattern leading upward.

Both girls set down their lanterns and began to examine each outcropping. A few moments later Jean exclaimed, "Here's a large stone that's loose!"

She tugged at it until the rock came away in her hand, and laid it on the floor of the passageway. Then she stood on tiptoe and peered into the empty space.

Louise hurried to her sister's side. "Do you see anything?" she asked, and held up her searchlight.

"Nothing in here," Jean said. "Oh, dear, I had

hoped that we would locate the missing codicil."

Louise came closer and peered into the niche herself. Did she imagine it or was there a piece of paper under the crumbling rock on the bottom of the niche? She reached in and pulled it out. The dusty object proved to be a folded, crumpled sheet of paper.

Quickly she opened it, and the two girls stared. Then they burst into laughter. Printed on it in English were the words, "So you got fooled, too!"

There was no signature, but both girls assumed that one of the many searchers during the past hundred years had written the note and left it there.

Jean became very serious. "Louise, do you suppose the person who wrote this found the codicil and tried to mislead other people on purpose?"

"If anyone did find it, he isn't honest or he would have brought it to the attention of the authorities," her sister replied, putting the message back in its niche.

Both girls were inclined to feel that the note had not been written by Karpalow or anyone helping him. The paper looked too old.

As the Danas continued to speculate on who might have discovered the codicil here, they heard a bell ringing in the distance. At first the girls wondered where it came from, but after listening closely, they decided that it was coming from the entrance to the passageway.

"We'd better go back and find out about it," Louise said.

She and her sister hurried along the dark corridor and finally returned to the main part of the cellar. Aunt Betty was standing there, a bell in her hand.

She said, "The police are here. They want to take you girls to the hospital to see an unconscious patient."

"Who is it?" Louise asked in surprise.

"They don't know. He's a stranger in town and has no identification on him."

"But why do they want us to see him?" Louise asked.

"Because you reported the presence of Uncle Ned's two attackers in town. The police think perhaps this man could be one of them."

"Oh, I hope he is," Louise said. "That would be great. Then we could have him arrested and perhaps even find out where the other sailor is."

Aunt Betty nodded. "Did you find anything?"

"Nothing but a joke," Jean said and told her aunt about the note. "Do you have any idea who may have put it there?" she asked.

Aunt Betty laughed. "Someone during the past hundred years. Maybe a member of the law firm or a former student."

When she and the girls reached the living room, Aunt Betty introduced her nieces to a police officer who was waiting.

"Louise, Jean," she said, "this is Officer Thomas. He'll take you to the hospital."

"We found the victim unconscious at the foot of the cliff," the officer told them. "Evidently he had been climbing up and lost his balance. From the description you gave us of the two men who attacked your uncle, we felt he might be one of them."

"We'll be glad to come with you and try to identify him," Louise said, and minutes later the three were being taken to the hospital by a young driver in a squad car.

"By the way," Officer Thomas said, "it seems that man Karpalow who had rented a box at the post office never used it after we staked out the place. We don't have anyone there now, but we're in touch with the people at the post office every day. So far no one has seen him."

"That figures," Louise said. "He knows the box is being watched and is taking no chances."

As the Danas walked toward the victim's room with Thomas, the officer said, "This man didn't have any identification on him so the hospital reported him to us. Apparently no one has inquired about him."

Just as the visitors reached the room, a nurse came out. She looked at them and said, "The patient is worse. He is sinking. I'm just going for help!"

CHAPTER VIII

"Stop Your Snooping!"

THE unconscious victim in the bed had so many bandages on his head that he was almost unrecognizable. Before the girls could get closer, an intern hurried in. He felt the man's pulse, then pulled a little box out of his pocket and removed a hypodermic needle from it.

"Would you mind stepping outside for a moment while I give the patient an injection?" he said to the Danas. "I'll talk to you later about this."

Louise, Jean, and Officer Thomas complied and waited in the corridor.

"Do you think he's one of the men you're looking for?" the officer asked the girls.

"Yes, but I can't be sure," Louise said. "He was lying on his side, and I couldn't see his left cheek. Did you, Jean?"

"No."

"Well, the scar is the only thing that will actually identify him."

Just then the doctor came to the door and motioned the callers inside. "This fellow had a nasty tumble," he said, "but I think he'll make it."

"The needle you gave him," Jean said. "Will it wake him up?"

"I think so. But his whole body is bruised, and he has several cuts on his head and face. He may not regain consciousness for some time."

As the doctor stepped away, Louise and Jean walked forward. The patient was now lying on his back. A moment later they looked at each other and nodded. On the victim's left cheek was an ugly scar! This must be Hoppy Canfield!

Louise said to Officer Thomas, "My sister and I think we recognize this man because of the scar on his cheek. He was a sailor on my uncle's ocean liner. He was discharged. We're not sure why he and his pal came to Still Harbor, but we surmise it was to injure us to get even with our uncle, Ned Dana."

They did not mention Karpalow or a possible connection between him and the two sailors, but wondered why Hoppy had been climbing up the cliff. Had he been planning to carry out some mischief on the girls or on the college, or even on Dr. Kenmore? Whatever the reason, Hoppy had failed and had injured himself in the attempt.

Suddenly the man in the bed sighed. The intern smiled. "The hypodermic is taking effect. Perhaps the crisis is over."

Everyone in the room watched the patient intently. Within a few seconds he began to mumble. The visitors moved closer and listened carefully to pick up the faint, jumbled words. At first they could make no sense out of them, but suddenly the man spoke several sentences loud and clear.

"Don't leave me, Lem! Lem, help me—Captain Dana, I'm not a crook. Lem talked me into this!"

The patient became quiet again, but Louise and Jean were excited. "There's no doubt but that he's Hoppy Canfield," Louise said. "His buddy is Lem Morehead."

The nurse returned to the room and the intern whispered some instructions to her. He nodded to the Danas and Officer Thomas, then left.

"I'm afraid I'll have to ask you to go," the nurse said to the visitors.

Before they could obey, Hoppy began to murmur again. This time no one could distinguish what the words were, except, "I want to go back to the *Balaska*, Lem. If you don't want to go with me, I'll go alone."

Louise turned to the officer. "Don't you think you should have a guard on duty day and night to catch anything else this man may say? Besides, there's a warrant out for his arrest in Oak Falls, where he assaulted Uncle Ned Dana. You wouldn't want him to escape."

"You're right," Thomas replied. "Nurse, please let these girls stay here until I return. I'll call headquarters. I'm sure they'll send a man here, and I'll stay until he comes."

After he had left, the nurse asked the Danas what he was talking about. They gave her a brief rundown on Hoppy Canfield. She knit her brow and said, "Is he apt to become dangerous? If so, I'd better strap him down."

The Danas did not know how to respond. Certainly Hoppy had done his share of the fighting when he and Lem had attacked Uncle Ned. Finally Jean said, "We don't know this man. You'd better ask Officer Thomas what he thinks."

The girls wished Hoppy would say something more and give them a clue as to whether or not he was involved in the mystery of the missing codicil. Just then Officer Thomas returned and Jean decided to try something.

Stepping beside the bed again, she said to the patient, "Hoppy, wake up! Hoppy, wake up!"

The man stirred and mumbled. "Oh—eh? What you want? I ain't heard reveille yet." The patient stopped speaking and seemed to go into a deep sleep.

Officer Thomas reported that a detective would come to relieve him. "In the meantime," he said, "the officer who drove us here will take you home. Thanks very much for coming. You've been a great help."

"Oh, we were glad to," Jean said. "Please let us know when we can see Hoppy again."

The officer promised to do so, and the girls said good-by to him and the nurse.

After they had climbed into the police car, the driver said, "Well, I hear from Thomas that you were able to identify the patient. So he's wanted by the police? Well, he's in a good safe place now and won't get out of our sight day or night. And if his buddy should find out where he is and come to see him, he'll be arrested at once."

When the girls reached home, they found Aunt Betty and Uncle Phil waiting for them. They were astounded to hear what had taken place in the hospital.

Dr. Kenmore remarked, "You did a great bit of work for the police."

"We enjoy being helpful," Louise said.

Aunt Betty asked, "Have you ever thought you'd like to be policewomen?"

Both nieces shook their heads, and Jean said, "No, we just want to remain amateur detectives."

The girls had just finished telling all the details of their latest adventure and Dr. Kenmore had gone back to his office, when the telephone rang. Louise, who was closest to it, went to answer the call.

A man's voice asked, "Is Dr. Kenmore there?"

"No, he's not," Louise replied. "Would you like to leave a message?"

Instead of replying, the caller asked, "Are you one of the Dana girls?"

"Why do you want to know?" Louise parried.

"Oh, I'm sure you are. And I just want to warn you. Stop your snooping, or something dreadful is going to happen to you and your sister!"

"What are you referring to?" Louise asked the man.

"Never mind," he replied, "but give your uncle this message. Tell him to make the deal with Mr. Karpalow, or he'll destroy the codicil and scatter the pieces to the four winds over the ocean."

Louise was angry. She asked the caller who he was. When he refused to tell her, Louise became more defiant. "We don't think Mr. Karpalow has the codicil. If he did, he wouldn't be silly enough to tear it up."

There was silence on the other end of the line for a few moments, then the caller said, "You do what I say, or Beacon College will never be able to benefit from what's coming to it." With that, the man hung up.

Louise stood by the phone for a few minutes, then returned to the others. She repeated the conversation word for word.

Jean said she thought the whole thing was just a hoax to get the money, but Aunt Betty looked worried. "Karpalow is still at it," she said with a sigh. "I wonder who sent the letter signed 'a former grounds keeper.'"

After luncheon the girls returned to the cellar. Cautiously they went to the spot where they had found the note.

"This is as far as we got before," Louise said. "I wonder where the corridor leads to from here."

"Let's find out," Jean urged.

Slowly the Danas proceeded through the dank passageway. Another curve lay ahead. Just as the girls were about to turn, they heard a loud scraping noise around the corner.

Louise and Jean stood still and listened, their hearts beating wildly. Everything was silent. The girls looked at each other and Jean was just about to say something, when they heard the noise again.

"Do you think someone besides us is down here in this cellar?" Jean whispered.

"I don't know," Louise replied. "If so, he must have heard us by now. So we may as well look." Bravely shining her flashlight ahead of her, she peered around the corner. The next moment she laughed.

"What is it?" Jean asked, glancing in the same direction.

"All I know is that something brown and furry disappeared into the wall when I shone the light on it," Louise replied. "Come on, let's see if we can find the hole."

There was, indeed, a small hole in the bottom of the wall. Louise poked into it, but found nothing. "It's probably the secret doorway of a mouse," she declared. "Nothing to worry about."

The girls went on and soon came to the end. If there ever had been an opening at this point, it was now sealed. They found nothing more and crossed off the cellar as one more bit of investigation accomplished, which unfortunately yielded no clues.

Soon after Dr. Kenmore had arrived home that afternoon, a special-delivery letter was brought to the front door. Aunt Betty signed for it and gave the envelope to her husband.

"It's addressed to you," she said.

He turned it over. "No return address," he remarked. "I wonder who sent it."

Aunt Betty became suspicious at once. "I hope it's not a threatening letter," she whispered.

Louise put an arm around her as they all waited for their uncle to open the letter.

CHAPTER IX

Warning in Flames

THE mysterious envelope was a long one. Inside was a small part of a sheet torn from a letter or document. It was old and brittle.

Dr. Kenmore laid it carefully on the living-room table. While the girls and Aunt Betty waited politely for him to read it, they noticed his puckered brow. He was puzzled over the contents.

Finally he said, "Come here and see this."

The other three crowded around the table and looked at the sheet. There was no question about its being very old. Scrawled on one line in old-time precise handwriting were the words, "Beacon College." Below it in barely legible writing the viewers made out the words, "treasure is valuable." Below this was a longer line. The ink, though faded, was quite readable. It said, "Follow the directions faithfully."

After reading it, Louise and Jean looked at their uncle. Louise asked, "Do you think it's authentic, Uncle Phil?"

"It certainly looks so," Dr. Kenmore admitted. "Maybe we've been misjudging Karpalow. Of course, he has no right to demand a hundred thousand dollars for the codicil when it never belonged to him in the first place. In any case, I don't propose to give the money to him."

"How can we find out whether this is authentic or not?" Louise queried.

Dr. Kenmore said he would take it to Professor Snyder in the morning. "He has several sidelines. One of them is testing old paper and ink for their age," he explained.

"That's great," Jean spoke up. "You won't have to take it far to find out."

Meanwhile, Louise had carefully picked up the old paper and held it up to a strong light. At first she tried to see through it, but this was impossible. Now she squinted at the topside of the paper and presently exclaimed, excited, "I'm sure the writing on this paper is recent!"

"How can you tell?" Aunt Betty asked.

Louise said she could see extremely faint markings on the paper, which she was sure had been the original ink. "It has been cleverly removed."

The others took turns looking at the scrap.

"You mean," said Aunt Betty, "that the person

who left this got hold of an old document, tore out this section, and removed what writing had been there?"

"Yes," Louise replied. "Then he faintly penned in his message, using brown ink, so it would look faded."

"That's very possible," Uncle Phil remarked. "But we still don't know whether this paper was part of the codicil. If it was, this section may have contained something that the extortionist didn't want me to read."

Dr. Kenmore went for a very fine magnifying glass, and the scrap of paper was carefully studied. He and his wife as well as the Dana girls concluded that there was no question about the nature of the paper. It was very old, but had a recent message on it, which probably had been written by Karpalow.

Uncle Phil pointed out that the last part could have a double meaning. "I mean the phrase, 'follow the directions faithfully,' " he said.

"But you're not going to do it," his wife reminded him, and he nodded.

"I'll have no dealing with any crooks!" he vowed.

It was decided that he and the girls would call on Professor Snyder early the following morning. "The discoveries we have made," the doctor said, "will coincide with his findings, I'm sure. The only thing I'm hoping is that he will be able to decipher what has been practically rubbed out. There must be a slight depression in the paper that can be traced."

At this moment they all heard a crash. It sounded as if it had come from the roof.

"What's that?" Aunt Betty cried.

"I'll find out," her husband offered and dashed up the stairway.

Louise and Jean rushed outdoors to see if a limb had broken off a tree and come down on the roof. They could not see one, but Jean suddenly detected a man in the distance, running very fast.

She turned to Louise, "You know what I think? Someone was listening to our conversation! He's probably one of Karpalow's spies, if not Karpalow himself. When he heard that his little trick had been found out, he angrily tried to do some damage here."

Before she finished speaking, the fleeing figure was out of sight, and the girls knew it was useless to pursue him. They entered the house just as Dr. Kenmore came down the stairs.

"I found a large rock on the roof," he said. "Someone must have thrown it up there."

The college president and the girls exchanged stories while Aunt Betty simply sighed. "I don't like the danger of this whole venture," she said.

The family stayed up a little later, waiting for the man to return, but he did not appear. Finally they all went to bed.

Louise and Jean had just dropped off to sleep, when they were awakened by the loud jangling of bells. They jumped up and rushed to the window. Not far away, one of the smaller buildings was on fire! Flames were leaping high into the air and within moments one part of the building after another started to burn and spurt up yellowish flames.

"That fire looks as if it had been deliberately set!" Jean exclaimed. "Let's see if we can help put it out!"

It was a noble thought, but proved to be hopeless. The girls had quickly jumped into slacks and shirts. They rushed from the house to the small building. By this time the campus fire apparatus had arrived and water was being pumped onto the flames. The whole area was too hot for the Danas to approach.

Within minutes the town fire-fighting units arrived and in a short time the spectacular blaze was put out. Louise and Jean walked over to where the town's fire chief and the college head of security were conferring.

"Was something combustible inside the building?" the fire chief asked.

"No, nothing was in there. I locked the place myself."

Louise and Jean walked up and introduced themselves. They described what they had seen from their bedroom window.

One of the smaller buildings was on fire!

"That sounds as if one or more persons put gasoline or something else flammable against the building and ignited several areas, so the fire would spread quickly," the fire chief said. "Have you any idea who might have started the blaze and why?"

Louise and Jean had their own opinion on this subject, but said they thought Dr. Kenmore should answer the question. He appeared shortly from the opposite side of the burned building and joined the group.

When the question was put to him, he said, "Frankly, I'm sure the fire was set on purpose. We have had threatening letters and phone calls from somebody who is trying to extort money from the college. We don't propose to pay it, and each time this stranger realizes I'm not going to change my mind, he seems to think of another frightening bit of deviltry."

The doctor turned to Louise and Jean. "Perhaps you had better run back to the house and tell Aunt Betty everything is all right."

The girls started off, but stopped suddenly. They could hear a low moaning sound near a grove of trees. Was someone hurt?

They listened carefully. Then, to their utter surprise, they could understand a trembling voice intoning, "Make—the—deal—with—Karpalow—or—suffer—a—worse—fire!"

The girls rushed forward into the grove, which

was partially lighted by the glowing embers. They saw no one and assumed that the person who had given the warning had disappeared. By this time Dr. Kenmore had caught up to them and was disturbed by their story.

"I think I'll have to double our security guard," he said.

Aunt Betty was upset by this latest development and was happy to hear that there would be more protection on the campus. "It will soon be time for all the students to arrive, and we don't want them to be frightened and perhaps decide to leave!"

Louise and Jean suddenly felt very weary and gladly went back to bed. By the time they came downstairs in the morning, Dr. Kenmore had already telephoned Professor Snyder for an appointment.

"He'll see us in about an hour."

After breakfast the three set off. Dr. Kenmore had the piece of old paper in his pocket. They told Dr. Snyder about the mystery, and he was eager to help them solve it.

First he put the paper under a strong microscope, enlarging the surface many times. Without divulging anything he saw, the expert went to a table and shelf in his lab, took down a bottle, and put a couple of drops of fluid on a soft cloth. He carried this back and rubbed the cloth on one little section of the paper. Finally he turned to the others and said, "The original writing is coming through faintly."

While his listeners waited in rapt attention, the professor continued to work, applying the specially treated cloth to the rest of the paper and watching through the microscope. Finally, he straightened up, smiled at his audience, and said, "I will tell you something amazing that should help you catch a thief!"

CHAPTER X

The Silent Prisoner

PROFESSOR Snyder asked when the scrap of paper had been delivered.

"Late yesterday afternoon," Dr. Kenmore replied, "Why?"

The professor said that only two days before a valuable old handwritten manuscript had been stolen from the college library. "Unfortunately, there was no copy of it and a microfilm had not yet been made."

Jean asked, "How could the manuscript have been stolen? Surely you must have a guard at the library, and at night the place must be locked up."

Professor Snyder nodded. "It's thought that whoever took the manuscript must be a slick thief. Neither the police nor others have been able to figure out how the person was able to get in. Furthermore, the manuscript was in a locked glass case and the key was not there. The glass was not broken, either."

The professor sighed and added, "You girls are detectives. How could it have been done?"

Louise said she could guess. "If the person is a clever thief, he might have brought tools, and taken the case apart without breaking anything. After removing the manuscript, he put the case back together again."

Dr. Kenmore remarked, "That's a great theory. No one else has mentioned it. You're probably right, Louise."

He asked the professor if anything else had been taken. The answer was no. The Danas immediately thought of the two men who had come to the library from another town, calling themselves professors. Could they have been phonies, working for Karpalow? And could they have returned to take the valuable papers?

Louise asked, "If the old manuscript was so valuable, why would the thief cut out part of it?"

The professor smiled. "I believe you said this crook has demanded a hundred thousand dollars from the college in return for information about the missing codicil. I doubt that the old manuscript would have brought that much."

The others were interested in this theory, but not knowing the value of the old papers, they could neither agree nor disagree. On one point they all had the same thought, however. The thief himself did not know the value of the document. He might have ruined something really precious.

Jean asked, "What do we do now?"

Dr. Kenmore replied, "I shall communicate with the police at once. I think they should get in touch with the Pleasant View authorities, and really comb that town."

Louise offered a suggestion. "It may be difficult for the police to trace Karpalow if he uses a different name wherever he's staying. Karpalow may be the one for the post-office box number only."

"You have a point there," Professor Snyder said, nodding.

Suddenly Jean had a thought. "Louise, why don't you and I go to the hospital to visit Hoppy Canfield? Perhaps he's better by this time and willing to talk. If he and his buddy Lem are really pals of Karpalow's, Hoppy might tell us what the man's real name is."

"Good idea," their uncle said.

The college president thanked the professor for his help, then drove into town. He dropped Louise and Jean at the hospital. He was going on to police headquarters to talk to the chief.

"We'll walk home," Jean offered.

As the Danas approached the injured man's room, they could hear music playing. Near the foot of Hoppy's bed stood a television set. A program was turned on.

When they looked at the patient, they received

a distinct surprise. Most of the bandages had been removed from his head and face, and he was propped up in bed with several pillows. He stared at the visitors as if he had never seen them before.

"Hello, Hoppy!" Jean said, smiling broadly at him.

Louise added, "It's good to see you feeling better."

The man continued to stare at the girls and said nothing. They wondered if he were all right physically but was suffering from amnesia. He did not act as if he recognized them.

To get him to speak, if possible, Louise said, "Has Lem been here to see you?"

The question seemed to pull Hoppy out of his forgetful state. "How do you know who I am, and who are you?" he asked.

The sisters glanced at each other, wondering how to answer his questions.

Louise decided that she would play it cool and not make any accusations against the sailor. Smiling, she said, "Oh, surely you remember us. We're Captain Dana's nieces."

Hoppy blinked. He looked away as if he were in deep thought. The girls waited for him to say something.

Finally he did. "So you're Captain Dana's nieces, and you came to see why I helped to attack him."

The girls waited for him to go on. When he remained silent, Louise and Jean began to feel disappointed. Was the man playing the part of someone in a semi-dazed condition who would answer them if he were able? Or was his condition worse than it appeared to be?

Louise walked over to the side of the bed and took one of Hoppy's hands in her own. "Wouldn't you like to get back on the *Balaska?*"

There was no answer. She went on, "I'm sure Captain Dana would forgive what you did and re-hire you if you would only tell the truth."

Hoppy hung his head. He did not try to pull his hand away from Louise's, and he gave every indication of being contrite. Unfortunately, he was apparently afraid to talk.

Jean came to Hoppy's bedside, and was about to ask him about Karpalow when a nurse walked into the room. She had been observing the scene from the hallway.

The nurse beckoned to the Danas to come outside, and said, "I have a suggestion for you. I think this patient is very confused. Why don't you leave your names and address. I have a hunch that Hoppy may take a while to think over what you said, and may very well ask to see you soon."

The girls agreed and the nurse wrote down their names and telephone number.

Louise said to her, "I'm amazed that Hoppy has such a deluxe private room."

The young woman smiled. "When he was brought into the hospital, there was no other bed available. Since his pockets were bulging with money, it was assumed he was well-to-do and could afford this kind of room."

The nurse went on to say that Hoppy was aware that he was being guarded day and night by the police and would make no attempt to get away.

"Furthermore, thinking about his situation, the patient might decide to tell you everything. Apparently his friend Lem has made no attempt to trace Hoppy's whereabouts."

The girls thanked the helpful young woman and then left the hospital. When they arrived home, the sisters learned from Dr. Kenmore that the police had no leads in the case. They admitted that they were puzzled about the thief who had stolen and purposely mutilated the old manuscript.

The college president now said, "I've decided to call a meeting of all the codicil searchers. The young couples are coming to the gazebo at eight o'clock."

When Paul and Deb arrived at the summerhouse, they went to sit on a bench with the Danas. The meeting was called to order, then Dr. Kenmore said, "I would like to hear from each couple what they have discovered."

The first person to speak was a boy named Roscoe. He was tall, lanky, and had bright-red hair. He grinned a good part of the time and turned out to be a humorist.

"My partner Sally and I," he began, "thought we had a hot lead at an old boathouse that's not used any more by the college. At first we started tapping the side walls from inside. None sounded any different from the rest—no thudding knocks or extra loud sounds. We were pulling on a closet door, when suddenly the whole thing gave way. Sally and I landed in the water!"

The others laughed.

"That wasn't bad enough," she took up the story. "That old boathouse was a hangout for muskrats. They didn't like us one bit and gave us a few nips."

A girl in the audience cried out, "Oh, goodness! What did you do?"

Roscoe grinned. "We got out as fast as we could!"

Dr. Kenmore asked, "So you didn't continue your search there?"

"Oh, yes, we did," Roscoe replied. "But we first dressed in armor-plated swimsuits."

Everyone grinned, then Roscoe added, "We told another couple about the place. They pursued the search."

"Chicken!" another boy cried out.

The couple, George and Trisha, who had taken over, stood up. George said, "We didn't mind because we did find a clue!"

All eyes turned in their direction. "In the attic of that boathouse," Trisha announced, "we found a little diary. It was old and dirty and the writing was faded. But you could make out some of it. We think it was written by John Beacon. One sentence read, 'Today I finished burying the treasure. But I feel very ill. I am afraid I may have injured my heart.'"

The Danas were astonished to hear this. Louise called out, "Don't stop there. Tell us what else it said!"

"That was about all," George replied. "But we thought it proved definitely that the treasure that is supposed to be mentioned in the codicil to Mr. Beacon's will is buried."

"But where?" a chorus of voices asked.

"Unfortunately, the diary didn't say," Trisha answered, and her listeners groaned in disappointment.

"Any other reports or guesses?" Dr. Kenmore asked the group.

When no one responded, Jean stood up. "Do you think that after John Beacon wrote in his diary that he had buried the treasure and felt ill, he went to bed and passed away?"

Louise said, "That would explain why no codicil was ever found. He couldn't write it until he buried the treasure, but he may never have had a chance."

Before anybody could comment on this theory, one of the girls in the group shrieked in terror and pointed to the entrance of the gazebo.

All eyes turned in that direction. A long, hissing snake was slithering into the building!

CHAPTER XI

Suspicious Motives

A SPLIT second after the search group saw the deadly snake wriggle into the gazebo, they jumped through the openings between the pillars. Apparently this was not to the reptile's liking. Its fangs shot out and it hissed again!

Most of the students ran away, but Louise and Jean stood nearby, watching. One couple, both zoology majors, remained just outside the enclosure.

After staring at the snake for a few seconds, the boy asked his partner, "Sue, isn't that a fer-de-lance?"

"Yes, Rudi."

Louise called to the couple, "Where do you think the snake came from? Surely it's not native to these parts."

"Oh, no," Rudi replied. "It comes from South America, and is really deadly."

Jean asked if someone should try to catch the reptile.

Sue replied, "By all means. I believe the fer-de-lance escaped from the college reptile house. I know there was one in it."

"How can you capture this poisonous snake?" Jean asked.

"With a large cage and several toads," Rudi answered.

Louise offered to hurry to a telephone and notify the college zoo keeper. "He'll be there, won't he?" she asked.

Sue nodded. "The man has a little apartment right next to the animals and snakes."

"Does he have a special phone number?" Louise asked.

"Call the college number and you'll be transferred to him," Sue replied.

Louise hurried to the nearest telephone and was soon in communication with the keeper, Mr. Garvin. He was amazed by her story and went to check.

He came back to the phone. "You're right! Somebody opened his cage door! I'll be over as soon as I get some things together."

By this time the fer-de-lance had crawled to the rafters of the gazebo and was gazing down balefully at his audience. It had stopped hissing and protruding its fangs.

Mr. Sam Garvin arrived with his little truck,

which had been especially built to carry wild animals. First, he took out a wire cage and set it at the doorway of the gazebo. Next, he reached into a covered box and pulled out a hoptoad. He held it by one leg, but let it struggle to get loose and attract the attention of the snake. The fer-de-lance reached down about a foot, as if to get the scent of the toad.

The zoo keeper now called Rudi over and asked him to hold the toad by the leg. The zoology student did as requested, then hurriedly introduced the keeper to Louise and Jean. Sam brought another toad from the box and moved a little distance away from the spot, nodding absently to acknowledge the introduction. He held onto this toad also, and looked up at the snake.

Louise and Jean watched in fascination. It was not until Sam had brought out five toads, three of which he let go, that the fer-de-lance made a move to come down from its lookout.

The watchers kept perfectly still. The snake swung its head from side to side, ready to detect any suspicious movement. Seeing and hearing none, and being acquainted with Sam, the fer-de-lance slowly dropped to the floor of the gazebo.

As the hungry reptile slithered toward Rudi, the boy let go of the toad. In a flash, the snake had devoured it. Now Sam let go of the toad he was holding. Again, the snake darted forward and swallowed it whole.

Louise and Jean wondered when Sam would try to capture the reptile. Again he reached into his box and brought out another toad. He let it hop through the bars of the snake cage from the rear, but held tightly to one of its legs. The temptation to devour it was too great for the fer-de-lance. Like lightning, it shot into the cage and ate the toad.

Rudi slammed the door shut and locked it. The trapped fer-de-lance began to hiss and expose its two fangs.

The Danas sighed with relief. They watched as Sam and Rudi lifted the cage onto the truck. The keeper thanked the boy for his help and then drove off.

Louise and Jean, Sue and Rudi walked into the gazebo and sat down. Louise asked, "How do you suppose the snake got loose?"

"Perhaps some careless student left the door open," Jean suggested.

"I doubt it," Sue replied. "Sam is very dependable. Knowing how dangerous the fer-de-lance is, he would make sure its cage was tightly locked."

"It looks," Rudi added, "as if someone had sneaked in there, deliberately opened the cage, then run off."

All this time Jean had been thinking about an idea she had. She told the couple that a man called Karpalow had been harassing the girls and Dr. Kenmore ever since the Danas had arrived.

"He has pulled all sorts of dangerous tricks on us," Jean went on. "We'd like to capture him, but so far we've had no luck."

Jean asked Sue and Rudi if they thought it was possible for Karpalow or one of his pals to have broken into the reptile house, opened the cage, and let the fer-de-lance out.

The couple agreed this was possible. Then Jean asked, "I understand snakes will follow the scent of an animal trail. Could Karpalow have deliberately made a trail scented with the meat of a small wild animal, perhaps a baby rabbit, directly to the gazebo?"

Rudi nodded. "Jean, do you think this man Karpalow overheard Dr. Kenmore call a meeting of the searchers and let the snake loose when the session was in full swing?"

"Yes," Jean replied. "It's just the kind of trick he would play. I wonder if he has been hiding somewhere nearby to see what would happen."

Rudi laughed. "I suppose he enjoyed watching everybody scatter, but he must have been disappointed that no one was bitten and that the snake was captured fairly easily."

Louise remarked that if Karpalow had really done this, he was certainly getting desperate. But why?

"Could it be that we're getting close to a solution of the codicil mystery and he's doing everything he can to keep us from finding it?"

The others thought this might be a reasonable assumption and tended to prove that the man was a faker. Was he determined to get the hundred thousand dollars before either the real codicil or the treasure was located?

Dr. Kenmore and a few searchers returned to the gazebo, but most of the others had gone to their dormitories. He praised Sue and Rudi for their presence of mind, and Louise for her dash to the telephone for help.

Early the next morning Dr. Kenmore received a phone call from a stranger, who said, "Deliver the scrap of paper from the codicil that you have to Hoppy Canfield at once."

When Uncle Phil told the others about the demand, everyone was amazed. "I wonder if that was Karpalow," Louise said. "If so, I'll bet this is his way of trying to find out where Hoppy is."

"I'm afraid you're right," said Aunt Betty, sighing. "Oh dear, I feel so uneasy. I'll be glad when this mystery is solved."

Her husband smiled. "I believe your nieces are tightening the net around that crook, and I have a feeling that it won't be much longer before they'll turn him over to the police."

Louise and Jean appreciated their uncle's compliment, but they felt that the remark was made mainly to quiet their aunt's fears.

The girls decided to go to the hospital at once and ask Hoppy what he knew about this latest demand. They borrowed Aunt Betty's car, but purposely took a circuitous route so they could not be followed. When they arrived at Hoppy's room, they found him seated in a chair. To their delight he looked up at them and smiled.

"Good morning," he said "I'm glad you came."

Louise said she was happy to see him apparently feeling much better. Then she asked, "Do you know anything about a phone call asking someone to bring a paper to you?"

Hoppy looked so utterly blank that the girls were convinced he knew nothing about it. They were not surprised at his reply. "I don't know what you're talking about."

He now asked the girls if they had spoken to Captain Dana yet about permitting him to return to the ship.

Louise said, "You'd really like to go back?"

"Yes."

Both girls were glad to hear this but decided to be cautious. Jean said, "We can help you to be reinstated if you'll just tell us the truth."

"About what?" Hoppy asked.

"About your connection with Lem," Louise replied.

The convalescent heaved a sigh, then said, "I'm paid by my buddy Lem to do jobs for him and not talk."

Jean said, "You mean like attacking my uncle?"

"Yes."

Louise put the next question to him. "Has Lem been here to see you, or has he phoned and tried to talk to you?"

"No. He doesn't know where I am, and I don't want him to find out."

Jean told Hoppy the girls were relieved at this decision. She then gave him the full story about the scrap of paper.

"I'm convinced that either Lem or Karpalow wants to find out where you are. You're in the safest place you could be if you want to sever your connection with those two men."

The prisoner-patient said he would be glad never to see either one again. "I almost got killed on account of them," he said.

"You mean when you fell down the cliff?" Louise asked.

Hoppy nodded, and Louise said, "Exactly what were you supposed to do when you got to the top of the cliff?"

Hoppy Canfield looked out the window for several seconds, then, turning back, he cast his eyes toward the floor. Finally he made up his mind to speak. "All right," he said, "I'll tell you."

CHAPTER XII

A Confession

BEFORE Hoppy Canfield began his story, Louise suggested that the police detective who sat in the corridor outside, guarding the room, be called in as a witness. The patient thought about this for several seconds, then said, "Yes. Perhaps it would be a good idea for the officer to come in."

Jean went into the corridor to summon the man, who brought in his chair.

"You know, it's your legal right to say nothing without the presence of an attorney," the officer told Hoppy. "Anything you say now may be held against you."

"I understand," Hoppy replied. "I don't feel I need a lawyer, because I haven't done anything really wrong. I'll tell you whatever I know."

"Okay," the officer said. "Go ahead."

"Lem and I had been buddies on the *Balaska* for a long time. Once, while we were in port in New

York, Lem met a man who calls himself Karpalow. That's not his right name—I never heard what it was. I don't know where he hails from.

"After Lem got back on the ship, he told me that Karpalow had a great scheme for getting a lot of money. If Lem and I would join him, he'd make it worth our while. Lem kept after me. When he got fired for knocking out one crew member and breaking another one's arm, I decided to go with him."

"And you didn't know what was expected of you?" Jean asked.

"Not at that point. I didn't like the idea of getting even with Captain Dana, but Lem insisted we go and 'teach him a lesson.'"

Louise looked at Hoppy disapprovingly, but he went on, "You can imagine how amazed he and I were, while spying on your house, to overhear that you girls were going to the same place where we were headed. That was just before we attacked Captain Dana.

"Lem immediately phoned Karpalow and told him about your visit to Beacon, but he said, 'Come on anyway. I know how to take care of the situation.'"

The *Balaska* sailor informed the Danas that when he and Lem had arrived at Pleasant View, he personally did not like Karpalow.

"I felt he was not a man to be trusted, but I was sort of caught in the scheme and didn't know how to get out of it. The arrangement was that Karpalow was to give Lem money and he in turn was to pay me. My getting paid depended on doing something—sometimes to Dr. Kenmore, sometimes to you girls—to cause trouble at the college.

"What kind of things were you to do at the college?" Louise asked him.

"We were to think up things to do and also we were given instructions. Karpalow planned the ghost stunt. Lem and I were chanters, and a friend of his played the ghost."

"Who was that friend?" Louise inquired.

"I only know his name is Pete," Hoppy replied.

"So he's the one who picked up Jean and was going to throw her down the cliff?" Louise went on.

"I think he was just hoping to scare her. He didn't mean to go through with it," the man replied.

"Hoppy," Jean said, "two men who looked like you and Lem were seen at the library."

"That's right. Karpalow sent us there. Wanted us to find out if there were any real old manuscripts—handwritten ones, and if so, where they were kept."

"And you told him?"

"Yes."

"Did you know why he wanted to find out?"

"No idea."

"Somebody loosened a stone on top of the cliff

the day we arrived. Jean almost fell down," Louise stated. "Do you know who did that?"

"No. Honestly, I don't," Hoppy said. "I only threw a rock on the Kenmore roof once to scare you."

"But you and Lem waited at the post office the day after Karpalow sent my uncle the first note," Jean continued.

"Right. He wanted to know if you had set a trap for him."

"How did he finally retrieve his letter?" Jean asked.

"I think he pretended to be one of the mailmen. He is a master of disguises."

"What does he really look like?" Jean asked.

"I can't tell you because I don't know. He has this thing about dressing up and appearing different each day. Sometimes he looks like an old woman and has a high, squeaky voice. At other times he is an old stoop-shouldered man, another time a tall, red-haired athlete. I think he gets a kick out of changing his looks so much. He's a little strange, anyway."

Jean changed the subject, "Who released the fer-de-lance at the reptile house?"

"I think it must have been Pete. I heard him talking about doing it."

Louise asked Hoppy, "The time you lost your balance on the cliff and were injured, what were you going to do on the campus?"

"I was to sneak up to Dr. Kenmore's house and

cause some kind of disturbance. Then I was to chant in a ghostly kind of voice, "Pay the money! Pay the money, or you will be attacked!"

There was a long pause, then the sailor said, "I'm glad I never got there. Now that I think about it, everything seems too silly. Karpalow must be crazy."

No one commented on that statement, but Jean said, "He seems smart enough to have figured out how he might get a hundred thousand dollars from the college."

"Maybe so," Hoppy agreed. "As soon as I can get out of here, I'm going to head straight to New York and try to get back on the *Balaska*."

The Danas looked toward the detective. Louise said, "After this confession, there wouldn't be any reason for holding Hoppy, would there be?"

"I'm not the one to say," the officer replied. "Someone with more authority would have to decide this. "But I will give a full report on what Hoppy told us a few minutes ago."

Louise thought the girls should leave now. No doubt Hoppy was tired.

"Before we go, Hoppy," she said, "will you please give us Lem's address?"

"Oh, I can't do that," Hoppy replied. "I couldn't squeal on a buddy, even if he is tied up with somebody who isn't honest."

The detective remarked, "It's possible that your buddy's story won't agree with yours and you can get into more trouble. If we know where he is, we can keep him from doing anything else to help Karpalow, and he may even lead us to the man."

Despite this advice, Hoppy could not be shaken from his resolve not to divulge his friend's whereabouts. The others gave up trying to persuade him.

Then Jean changed the subject. "As soon as we reach Dr. Kenmore's, we'll try to get in touch with our uncle Ned and see if he will let you come back."

On the way home, the sisters decided to go to the library and study more about the Vikings. For about an hour both girls read silently.

Then Jean said, "Let's go! I'm tired of reading."

When they arrived at the Kenmore house, Louise sent a cable to Uncle Ned. Then the two girls discussed what they might do next to solve the mystery. They eliminated further search around the campus because others on the team were busy trying to find the missing codicil.

Jean asked her sister, "Do you feel daring enough to try going down the cliff to see if we can find something on the hillside?"

"I'm game," Louise replied, "but I'd hate to get hurt the same way Hoppy did."

The girls decided to put on sneakers with corrugated rubber soles to keep them from slipping. When the Danas reached the cliff, they walked along the rim, hunting for the spot that would be the least dangerous to descend. As they went on, the cliff seemed to become steeper. Finally they turned around and went back to the section beyond the end of the new fence.

"All right, here goes," Jean said.

The girls stepped down from the rim. They soon decided that it would be advisable either to turn around and go down backward or to take a few steps to the right, then to the left, zigzagging all the way to the bottom. Jean chose the latter, Louise the former. There was far less chance of losing one's balance.

The Danas inched their way along, stopping every couple of feet to survey their surroundings.

Suddenly an idea hit Louise. "Jean, if we go on like this, we'll never be able to really check out the whole cliff."

"You're right," her sister admitted. "Suppose instead of going straight, we work our way down in a spiral pattern, covering about half of the cliff each time. Then, when we come up again, we can do the same thing, examining the other half. It'll take a lot longer, but we won't miss anything."

"That's a great idea," Jean said. "Just be careful. There are a million loose stones here. We could easily lose our footing and slip."

Meticulously the sisters examined the cliff, looking under rocks to see if something was hidden there. They felt into crevices and poked into mounds of earth. They found nothing.

After a while Louise sat down to rest. "It seems

almost hopeless," she said with a sigh. "But I think we should go on."

She turned to look at the harbor and noticed that the water level had changed.

"The tide's coming in," she said. "That really looks rough!"

"And it has a terrible backwash!" her sister added.

The two girls got up and continued to climb down. This time they held hands. Suddenly Louise let go of Jean's hand. She had seen a bush under which she thought something might easily have been hidden. As she yanked it, Louise lost her footing.

"Oh!" she cried out.

Louise reached wildly for Jean but to no avail. The next moment she was rolling pell-mell down the side of the cliff toward the choppy water!

CHAPTER XIII

A Risky Swim

As Louise rolled down the almost vertical cliff, Jean was horrified. She could not possibly reach her to help.

Instead, she yelled, "Grab a bush! Oh, Louise, quick! Quick! Grab a bush!"

Louise was terrified but did not lose her presence of mind. She heard her sister's frantic instructions. There was not much vegetation on the cliff, which was covered with loose stones.

Finally she did spot one fairly large shrub directly ahead of her. If she caught the bush in her hand, would she tear it loose? She was afraid but undaunted. Louise deliberately tried to roll toward it and use the mass of stalks and stems as a stop.

Her plan worked. Despite the speed with which she hit the bush, it held fast. The exhausted girl lay there, panting, scraped, and bruised.

In a few moments Jean scrambled to her sister's

side. "Thank goodness you're all right!" she said. "You had me scared to death!"

Louise gave a wan smile. "I was pretty scared myself. It's lucky the bush was there."

As soon as Louise had risen and brushed the dirt from her clothes, the sisters once more began to inch their way down the rest of the cliff. When they reached the shoreline, the girls walked first in one direction, then in another, hunting for any kind of clue to the buried treasure.

Finally Jean said, "If it's anywhere around here, there should be some kind of a marker."

Unfortunately neither of the girls could see anything, either along the shore or partway up the cliff, that gave a hint of a probable site.

When the girls had started down, the tide had been low, but now it was coming in fairly fast.

"I'm hot," Jean said finally. "Let's take off our sneakers and roll up our jeans. Then we can walk into the water and keep on hunting."

As soon as they were ready to wade in, Jean noticed that a short distance out water was splashing against an object protruding from the rocks and sand. Could it be part of the vessel that had broken up here long ago, or was it from a more recent shipwreck?

Jean splashed through the water as quickly as possible. When she reached the object, the girl sleuth found it to be another stela. Excited, she looked at it, then called to Louise, who was some distance away.

"Come here! I've found a stela with faint markings on it. I'm sure they're runic."

Louise started toward her sister, but realized that the inrushing tide made it almost impossible for her to keep her footing. Finally she did manage to come within a few feet of Jean.

At this instant a huge rock sailed through the air and landed between the two girls! The splash it made knocked Louise and Jean off balance. But as they were about to go underwater, both of them glanced up to the top of the cliff.

A man stood there with his arms outstretched, as if he had thrown the rock!

He wore a cap pulled low, so that it was impossible to distinguish his features. By the time the girls had regained their footing and could stand up, the stranger had vanished.

"I wonder if that was Karpalow," Louise sputtered.

"I doubt it," Jean said, shaking the water out of her hair. "According to Hoppy, he never does any of his dirty tricks himself. He has other people do them for him."

"And a dirty trick it was!" Louise said angrily. "We were lucky that rock didn't hit either of us. I wonder if he meant to hurt you and me or just scare us. What do you think?"

When Jean did not reply, Louise turned around. Her sister was being swept up by a huge breaker! Then Louise too was toppled by an incoming

A huge rock landed between the two girls!

wave. She floated into shore as far as possible, then stood up. Her attempt to wade the rest of the way was useless, however. The undertow pulled her backward and sent the girl toward the sea!

Louise and Jean began to fear they were losing the battle against the water. They decided not to try standing up again, but to swim toward shore. Again and again they were swept back.

Louise had managed to stay close to the shoreline, but Jean seemed to be getting farther and farther away.

"Jean! Jean! Come back!" Louise shouted.

When she saw that her sister's struggles to come straight into shore were futile, she cried out, "Try swimming toward the far shore. That's the way the waves are heading!"

A sudden thought came to Louise. She was near the stela. Why not try to get there and hold on to it?

"Then I'll tell Jean to head for it, too."

Though she struggled against the unruly waters, it took Louise much longer than she had expected to reach the stone. Then she looked across the water. Jean was still battling the strong tide. There was not a boat of any kind in view that they might signal.

Louise thought hopelessly, "This is known as a dangerous harbor. No boat would come into it at high tide!" She looked up at the cliff. No one was in sight.

Louise clung desperately to the stela, and tried to signal her sister. Jean looked exhausted. She had given up the fight and turned onto her back to try resting a little before swimming any more.

"Oh, don't give up!" Louise pleaded, shouting as loudly as she could to be heard above the roar of the water.

Apparently Jean caught her sister's plea and began to backstroke toward the shore. Waves broke over her face. She floated again.

"I'll have to take a chance and go help her," Louise thought.

She felt a bit revived by this time and set out. The distance between the girls was not great, but the water crashing heavily against rocks, blinding the pair, made a meeting almost impossible. With superhuman effort, Louise reached her sister's side and grabbed one hand. Then she turned and started swimming toward the stela.

The move seemed to give Jean new courage. In a moment she turned over and began to swim alongside Louise.

Finally the two reached the stela and clung to it, despite the rough waves, which seemed bent upon sweeping them away.

A full minute went by, then Louise asked, "Do you think we can get to shore?"

"I'll try in a minute," Jean replied. "But—I'm—all—in!"

CHAPTER XIV

Pursuit of a Suspect

THE Danas held onto the stela in the bay as long as they could, resting and trying to relax. The incoming tide, however, finally covered it entirely. There was nothing left for the girls to do but swim to shore.

"I'm getting cold," Jean said, shivering. "I can't stay here any longer without turning into an icicle."

"The exercise will warm you up," Louise said. "Come on, we'll swim with the tide and get to shore somewhere, probably not where we went in."

Both girls set out. Though the distance was not far, it seemed like a mile because the undertow carried them back one stroke for every two strokes they took forward. Finally a huge wave overtook them and literally slammed them ashore a few hundred feet from the spot where they had started out. They grabbed hold of nearby rocks and pulled themselves up as the water rushed out to sea again. Louise and Jean lay exhausted for a few minutes, breathing heavily. After they had recovered a bit, the girls pulled themselves up even higher to a safe place, and lay down in the sun to dry.

Their good spirts and energy soon returned, and finally Jean said, "We'll have to climb up again. Shall we go straight or in a spiral, so we can examine the second part of the cliff?"

Louise laughed. "Haven't you had enough yet?"

"Well, I feel much better. How about you?"

"I'm willing. Let's go!"

The two girls walked along the bottom of the cliff to the area they wanted to cover, looking for their sneakers on the way. The rubber-soled shoes, however, were gone!

"The waves must have carried them away," Louise surmised.

Suddenly Jean said forlornly. "You're right. Look out there! Our shoes are floating away."

Louise said hopefully, "Maybe the tide will bring them in and deposit both pairs on the shore. We can come back later and pick them up."

Jean smiled. "You're an optimist, all right. Well, I suppose we'd better start our climb up the cliff."

The girls went cautiously, trying to avoid loose pebbles and little bushes with prickles on them. The part of the cliff they were surveying now was almost bare of vegetation and had few large rocks or crevices, so they spent less time examining it.

Suddenly Jean cried out, "Ouch!"

"What's the matter?" Louise asked her.

"A crawly creature just ran across my foot and stung me!"

"You'd better sit down and put some mud on it," Louise advised.

She went to her sister's side. Louise scooped up a little of the hillside dirt, wrung out part of her blouse onto it, and made a cake of mud in the palm of her hand. Then she slapped it over the sting.

"Thanks," said Jean gratefully. "Well, we can't say we haven't had any adventures today. I think I'll be glad to get home and out of these wet clothes."

Jean thought that perhaps the cake of mud would not stay on her foot as she continued to climb, so she pulled a sodden handkerchief from her pocket and tied it around her foot. Then she and Louise climbed higher.

Out of breath, they finally reached the top and sat down to rest. Ten minutes later they started off and arrived, footsore and muddy, at the Kenmore home. They went to the kitchen door and rang the bell.

Aunt Betty came to answer it and looked at the girls aghast. "What in the world happened to you?" she asked, opening the screen door.

"It's a long story," Louise replied. "We'll tell

you as soon as we've had baths and shampoos. Aunt Betty, would you mind bringing us our robes and slippers so we won't track this muddy water through the house?"

Mrs. Kenmore hurried off and soon returned with the robes and slippers. In a corner of the kitchen, the girls exchanged their wet clothes for the dry ones, and hurried upstairs.

Louise called back, "Aunt Betty, please don't touch our things. As soon as we're dressed, we'll take care of them."

Mrs. Kenmore did not reply. She smiled, picked up the soggy bundle, and went to the basement with it. A few moments later it was in the washing machine.

By the time Louise and Jean came downstairs, Aunt Betty had a snack ready for them. As they ate it, the girls related what had happened to them.

Louise ended the story by saying, "We did make a valuable discovery, though. We found a stela in the bay, exactly like the one in the gazebo. Do you suppose John Beacon could have hidden the treasure under it, using the stela as the marker?"

Aunt Betty thought this over. "I doubt it," she said. "I think any kind of treasure would be ruined by being underwater for so long. Besides, as the tides come and go here, they shift the earth. What might have been buried under the stela a hundred years ago, probably wouldn't be there now."

Jean told her aunt about the man on the cliff who had heaved the huge rock into the water. "We think he may have intended to injure us," she said. "We can't figure out why, though."

Mrs. Kenmore was disturbed by this news. "I'll have to ask my husband to triple the number of guards on the campus. This sort of thing must not be allowed to go on!"

Louise said that in the meantime she would like to go back to the top of the cliff and hunt for clues to the stone thrower. She and Jean left after promising their aunt they would not do anything dangerous. At the edge of the cliff they tried to gauge the spot from which the rock had been thrown.

At first they were not sure where it was, then Jean spotted a deep, somewhat rounded depression in the ground.

"I'm sure this is where the rock was," she declared. "One thing is certain—the man who lifted this and threw it such a distance must be very strong."

Louise agreed and began searching the ground for clues to his identity. Not far from the spot she saw a ball-point pen on the ground. She picked it up and turned the pen around. One one side were the initials P. T. O.

As Louise stared at the pen, she said, "I wonder if this belongs to the stone thrower or to one of the students or faculty here."

Jean suggested that there was one way to find out. "Let's go to the registrar and see if anyone who is connected with Beacon college has these initials."

Mr. Brady was in charge of the office that day. He heard the girls' story and examined the pen. Then he opened the college's directory and hunted for a name with the initials P. T. O.

Finally he closed the book and looked up. "Sorry, girls," he said, "I'm afraid I can't help you. No one working at or for the college has those initials."

The Danas thanked him and turned to leave. Suddenly Mr. Brady cried out, "Wait! A thought just came to me."

The sisters went back, and the registrar said that he remembered an ad that had come to his office. "These pens with someone's initials on them were to be given free with a year's subscription to *Merit Magazine*."

Jean was intrigued by this clue. "You think possibly a new subscriber might have the initials P. T. O.?"

Mr. Brady said yes and offered to telephone the magazine at once.

"That would be great," Louise said. "But don't let on that the person who owns the pen is under suspicion."

Mr. Brady smiled. "I understand."

He was on the telephone for several minutes

before he said, "Thank you very much." He wrote something on a paper, then hung up.

The registrar held up the paper for the Danas to see. "I never thought of myself as a detective, but maybe I uncovered a clue for you!"

On the sheet was the name Peter T. Osterbridge and an address.

"He lives in Pleasant View and recently subscribed to *Merit Magazine*," Mr. Brady said.

"That's a great clue!" Jean exclaimed.

The Danas thanked him and left. On the way home, Louise said suddenly, "Jean, something just occurred to me!"

"What?"

"Peter Osterbridge could be the man Hoppy referred to as Pete."

"You're right," Jean said. "I doubt that Karpalow has two buddies named Peter. That would be too much of a coincidence."

When the girls arrived at the Kenmore home, they told Aunt Betty the news, then borrowed her car and drove to police headquarters. By this time all the men on the force of the little town of Still Harbor knew the girls.

The officer on duty, Sergeant Thomas, smiled and asked what he could do for them. They showed him the pen they had found and the name and address of the owner.

"We suspect he's the man who threw a huge rock from the campus cliff into the bay, almost hitting us while we were in the water," Jean explained.

"And you think this person might have a police record?" the officer asked.

"Yes," the girls replied.

The sergeant called in another man and asked him to bring the file of wanted criminals.

Shortly he said, "Ha-ha, you girls had a good hunch. Here is a Peter Thomas Osterbridge, who is wanted by the police for armed robbery in Pennsylvania." The officer sobered. "If he is in this vicinity, we'll make every effort to find him."

He asked the Danas to step behind his high desk and look at a photograph of the man. Since they had not seen his face, they could not identify him. Both girls were sure, however, that he was a member of Karpalow's gang. Louise mentioned this to the sergeant, who said he would telephone a report to the Pleasant View police at once.

After that, he said to the girls, "I'll put a special stakeout near the place where you found the pen. It's possible that Peter Osterbridge will go back there to look for it."

"I hope you catch him," Louise said as the girls got ready to leave.

They drove home. By this time Dr. Kenmore had arrived. He and his wife were amazed to hear the latest string of clues. They did not feel too hopeful that the wanted man would be caught.

Uncle Phil said, "He's probably far too slick

for that. What interests me more is, if he is the one who threw that rock at you, why did he do it?"

Discussion on this subject lasted several minutes. Everyone was convinced that all the clues were connected, but the question was, how did one go about putting them in place?

Aunt Betty said cheerfully, "Don't worry! I'm sure everything will come out all right in the end." She grinned. "All right for everyone except the villains."

Later in the afternoon Sergeant Thomas phoned. Louise answered.

"I'm afraid I have bad news for you," Thomas said. "The Pleasant View police went to Oster-bridge's address but it looks as though he's flown the coop. His landlady said he moved out days ago. She thinks he's still in this area, so I'm sure he dropped the pen. But wherever he is so far he hasn't returned for his pen."

"That's too bad," Louise said. "I do hope he'll show up sooner or later. Thanks for keeping us informed."

After spending the rest of the afternoon in the college library, reading more about Viking history, the girls returned to the Kenmore house just in time for supper.

The family had just finished eating when the doorbell rang. The callers were Paul and Deb. After formal greetings with the college president and his wife, the couple said hello to the girls, and then suggested that they go out on the porch to talk.

When everyone was seated, Deb said, "We searched and searched for the missing codicil."

"And did you come up with a good clue?" Louise asked hopefully.

Both Deb and Paul shook their heads, but Paul said, "We have something new to track down and need your help. How about it?"

CHAPTER XV

The Hidden Skeleton

DEB and Paul spoke in whispers so that no eavesdroppers could hear what they were saying. Louise and Jean leaned forward, listening intently.

"We've located a hidden cave," Paul said.

Deb added, "The entrance was entirely covered with bushes and we almost missed it. The place is huge inside!"

"Where is the cave?" Jean asked.

"On the far side of the cliff, about one third of the way down from the top of the hill. It's a steep incline but fortunately it doesn't end in the water. You can walk on and on."

Jean whispered, "How far in did you go?"

Paul said not far, because they had not brought flashlights with them and could not see very much beyond the entrance.

"So you have no idea how long the cave is or what it may contain?" Louise asked.

"Not the slightest," Deb replied, "but maybe we'll discover the missing codicil inside."

Louise and Jean were eager to join the search and were glad their friends had invited them to go along.

"When do you want to start exploring?" Louise asked.

"Right after breakfast tomorrow morning," Paul answered. He grinned. "Don't be late!"

It was finally arranged that Paul and Deb would pick up the girls at nine o'clock. They were waiting when the couple arrived.

"Morning," said Jean. "I wasn't sure how one should dress for a trip to a cave. How do you like this getup?"

Both she and Jean wore old jeans and long-sleeved shirts with the collars buttoned tightly. Their heads were covered with dark-colored scarves. Each girl carried a pair of dark gloves.

Deb laughed. "You look like gypsies," she said.

Paul added, "Or a couple of cave dwellers protecting their hair from bats!"

The others smiled, then Deb said, "You do look kind of funny, but you're more sensibly dressed than I am. Have you an old scarf and a pair of gloves you can lend me?"

Louise produced a scarf but had to ask Aunt Betty for an extra pair of gloves. They also brought a pair of Dr. Kenmore's for Paul.

The young man pretended to feel neglected.

"Aren't you afraid of something happening to *my* hair?"

Before he could say he was joking, Louise dashed back into the house and came out with a large, dark-red handkerchief. "You may as well play gypsy, too," she declared, handing him the bandana. Deb helped him put it on, and the four searchers went off.

The Danas found that the hillside under which the cave was located was not so steep or rough as the cliff. It was fairly easy to keep one's balance going down.

When the group reached a certain spot, Deb and Paul stopped. Beside them was a huge clump of bushes, so thick and intertwined that one could not see through them. Deb and Paul reached up and grabbed the topmost branches. By swinging on them, they managed to turn them down far enough to reveal the opening to the cave.

"Go on in," Paul directed the Danas.

The sisters hurried inside, and Deb followed. Then the girls leaned forward against the bushes until Paul could worm his way into the cave. Each one in the group carried a large lantern with a strong beam that lighted the cave as if it were midday.

The four beams were cast over the ceiling, down one side wall, across the floor, and up the other side.

Louise remarked, "This cave doesn't look rough enough to be natural. It seems man-made."

Jean suggested that there may have been a smaller cave, which had been enlarged for some reason.

"Like what?" Deb asked.

"Oh, for people to live in."

"You mean Indians?"

"Who knows," Louise said, shrugging.

The searchers went very slowly, so they would not miss an inch of the space they were investigating. The floor was earthen and unusually smooth for a cave. Again it seemed as if it must have been man-made. There were outcroppings of moss and tiny crawling vines, which clung precariously to the rocky sides.

The Danas and their friends walked for about ten minutes without finding anything suspicious, not one removable rock or opening of any kind. There was nothing to give them a clue to the hiding place of the missing codicil.

Finally they came to a spot where a rock had once been painted red. Paul tugged on it with all his might, then Jean and Deb tried to help him. The rock would not move.

During the past few minutes, Louise had walked on ahead. The tunnel made a slight curve. When she went around the bend and beamed her light, the young sleuth gasped.

"Oh!" she cried out. "Come here, everybody!"

Seated on the ground with his back against one wall was a skeleton!

Jean, Deb, and Paul hurried forward. When they saw the bony figure, they too gasped, astonished.

Paul went closer and played his strong light directly on the skeleton. He remarked, "It's real, all right—not plastic. Once upon a time, that skeleton was part of a human being!"

"He gives me the shivers," said Deb. "How do you suppose the skeleton got here?"

Each of the others had a different guess. Paul said, "Maybe he was murdered and brought here!"

Jean remarked, "My guess is he was an Indian and perhaps was left here to die. I'll bet he's been here a long time."

Louise spoke up. "Yes, a very long time. I could even imagine he was once a Viking sailor. But someone since then has handled him. See, he's wired together."

The four young people decided to go farther. As they walked along, the searchers kept talking about the skeleton.

"There are no clues as to who he was," Louise remarked. "No bits of hair, or clothing, or anything to go by."

Deb remarked, "This is a terribly gruesome conversation. Let's talk about something pleasant."

"What do you suggest?" Paul asked her.

"How about me?"

"We'd better not start that," Paul teased her. "You might be sorry."

After that, there was silence for some time. Flashlights beamed to the left, right, overhead, and on the ground. The searchers could see nothing unusual but they went on.

Suddenly Jean stopped the group and said, "I have an idea. Do you suppose old Mr. John Beacon could have left the skeleton as a guidepost to the missing codicil?"

The others considered this point. It seemed valid enough, but there was nothing about the bony figure against the wall to indicate any directions to follow.

"There was no sign of loose stones or anything around it," Paul said.

The group walked on in silence for several more minutes, then suddenly Jean said, "Listen!"

"Did you hear something?" Deb asked her.

"I think I hear water!"

Everyone listened intently and said Jean was right. They hurried on through the cave. After several more twists and turns, they could see the end of it. The opening was much smaller than the one through which they had come. Splashing up against it was turbulent water.

"This must open onto the bay," Louise said.

"I wonder how long it has been here. It's odd that no one at the college has mentioned it to us or to the other searchers."

Jean said, "At high tide, this entrance must be entirely under water."

"What I want to know," Deb spoke up, "is who used it and for what purpose."

They could only guess. Louise said, "I'll bet the Vikings knew about it. They may have used it as a hideaway when under attack by Indians."

Paul remarked that it could be the other way around. "Maybe Indians knew about it and hid in here to protect themselves from the Vikings."

As the four searchers discussed what seemed to be an unsolvable question, Deb suddenly noticed that the tide was coming in.

"We'd better hurry back!" she said. "We don't know how far up the tide may run in this cave. I don't fancy being drowned in such a place."

The others did not argue. They realized that they had been going downhill and now found themselves plodding back up. Paul began looking for watermarks on the side of the cave.

"The stones down here are much lighter in color than the ones up above," he observed. "I suppose the water washes off whatever dirt is on them."

At just about the point where the skeleton was seated, the waterline suddenly stopped.

Paul said, "Whoever put the skeleton in that spot must have known about the tide level in here and didn't want the figure to be washed away."

"Just the same," Deb remarked, "I'd rather be out of this cave, water or no water. We haven't found any clue to the missing codicil, so let's go."

The others agreed, though all of them said they were disappointed that they had not found one single clue. They walked on, but there was no conversation. Thoughts were racing through everyone's head, but each felt that what he was thinking was not worth mentioning to the others.

Jean was at the head of the search party. As she approached the entrance, the girl detective suddenly stood still and put up her hand, signaling for the others to pause. They did.

"What's up?" Louise whispered.

"Shh!" Jean replied in a low tone. "I think I just heard some men!"

Everybody froze and listened attentively. There were voices outside the cave—men's voices. But their conversation was too muffled for those inside to understand a word.

The four in the cave looked at one another, gripped by cold fear. Were their enemies about to come in?

"We should have posted a guard," Louise finally said in a desperate whisper. "I'm sure Karpalow's men followed us!"

"What are we going to do?" Jean asked. "There isn't any place to hide in the cave as far as I can remember."

"And we can't go out the other end," Deb said haltingly. "If we try it, we'll drown!"

"Maybe that's their scheme," Jean said. "They might have trailed us and waited until we entered the cave, and now they won't let us out!"

A cold chill went down the Danas' spines.

"You mean," Deb asked in a barely audible voice, "that we're going to die?"

CHAPTER XVI

Worrisome Wait

THE Dana girls and their friends Deb and Paul slowly but cautiously moved near the hillside entrance of the cave. Were one or more persons about to come inside and attack them? They strained their ears to hear what was being said. It was impossible. The group outside did not move.

Louise thought, "I wonder if they're discussing what they should do."

"I think we ought to go back through the cave," Deb whispered. "We might be caught by some of Karpalow's men and never get out of here!"

"Yes, and we might also be trapped by the water!" Jean reminded the others. "But let's try it."

On tiptoe the group retraced their steps. They went to the turn before pausing.

"This is as far as I think we should go," Jean

said. "In a little while the water will be up to this point."

They had extinguished their lights, but now Louise turned hers on and beamed it around. Suddenly she exclaimed in a hoarse whisper, "The skeleton is gone!"

"But how could it be?" Paul asked. "We were here just a few minutes ago. Surely no one could have entered the cave from the bay side without our knowing about it!"

Louise looked concerned, and Jean said, "There must be a spook in here."

She too turned on her flashlight and examined the footprints around her. She recognized hers and Jean's, then looked at the sneakers Deb and Paul wore. She traced the tracks. There was one extra set of shoe prints! They led down the cave but within seconds were lost because by this time the water had covered them.

"Someone must have come in here from the bay," Louise announced. "But I don't see how he could do it without drowning!"

Deb heaved a sigh. "It seems as if so many of our theories end nowhere, and we are just more puzzled," she said. "Perhaps we'd better go back the other way, and see if those mysterious people have left."

They turned around, but Louise and Jean kept thinking about the strange shoe prints. Definitely they belonged to a man. But who was he? Someone who had stolen or borrowed the skeleton to scare the girls, having learned they were coming into the cave? And did he know of a secret hiding place? If so, why couldn't the young people find it?

Since there seemed to be no answer, the group hurried forward to the hillside entrance. As they tiptoed closer to it, Deb suddenly began to laugh. The others looked at her in astonishment and asked what was so funny.

"I recognize my friend Julie's voice outside," she replied. "The mysterious people we were afraid of must be other searchers!"

"But the voices we heard before were men's," Jean objected.

"Some of the boys may be with her," Deb said. "Anyway, I'm sure it's safe for us to leave here. And to tell you the truth, I can't wait to get out!"

When they parted the bushes and emerged, the other search couples jumped in utter amazement.

Julie cried out, "Where did you come from?"

Jean grinned. "Ladies and gentlemen, it will cost you nothing to enter the cave of the skeleton."

"What do you mean?" Julie asked.

Deb explained, then Julie remarked, "But you said the skeleton has been stolen. How can we see it if it isn't there?"

Jean was still grinning. "That's the question. Perhaps you can find the thief."

Julie's answer was, "No, thanks!"

Deb, Paul, and the Danas gave a brief description of their adventure. The listeners were intrigued by the idea that the far end of the cave was practically under water; and during high tide water rushed some distance into the cave.

"Of course," said Louise, "the cave isn't straight, so the distance the water would have to come to reach the level in the bay might not be so great."

Paul suggested that the skeleton might have been stolen from the biology laboratory, and said, "Why don't we all go over there and find out?"

"Good idea," the Danas said.

They all trooped to the science building. Here they were told that neither a skeleton nor anything else was missing.

"My clue petered out," Paul said, disappointed.

Next they went to the medical building and inquired about skeletons they might have there. A nurse at the desk looked at the group as if she thought they were playing a joke on her.

With a twinkle in her eye she said, "We don't have walking skeletons around here. Is there anything else you'd like?"

Paul, who knew her, laughed and assured her the group was serious. "We suspect someone stole a skeleton and hid it in a cave. Would you mind checking to see if all your skeletons are here?"

The nurse picked up her phone and dialed a

number. She made the inquiry and after receiving an answer, hung up and turned to the waiting group.

"All the skeletons that belong here are in their proper places," she said.

"Well, thanks a lot," Paul said. "Come on, everybody, we'll have to hunt somewhere else."

The searchers left the building but stood outside, discussing the problem. "Do you suppose," Jean asked, "that the skeleton could be privately owned?"

Louise said she was sticking to her original theory that the skeleton had been in the cave for a long, long time and had only recently been discovered.

"Possibly the person who took it was afraid we might carry it off. If he borrowed the skeleton, he would not be able to return it."

In a little while the group separated. The Danas went back to the Kenmore home, reaching it just around lunchtime. As they entered the front hall, the telephone rang. Louise answered it.

"Ken!" she said, excited. "And hi, Chris!" she added.

As Louise motioned Jean to come forward, she talked to the boys. Then both sisters listened to their friends. They were delighted to hear that the boys would arrive that very evening if it was convenient for the Kenmores to have them.

Jean went to check with her aunt, then replied, "Yes, indeed. What time will you arrive?"

"We'll be there by seven," Ken replied. "Maybe earlier."

Jean spoke. "It'll be great to see you both, and we have so much to tell you about the mystery."

"Great!" Chris said. "We have to set off now. It's a long way to Beacon College. See you later."

"Take it easy!" Louise advised. "Watch out for drivers who think they own the road."

"Don't worry," Ken assured her. "We'll both get there in one piece. Good-by."

Chris chimed in, "Good-by for now!"

Louise put down the phone, then both girls went to talk to the Kenmores about the visitors.

Aunt Betty smiled. "Tell me what their favorite dessert is, and I'll make it."

Louise and Jean thought a few seconds, then Jean said, "They like hot apple crisp with a nice big scoop of vanilla ice cream on top."

"Then that's what they'll get," Aunt Betty said.

After lunch, Louise and Jean helped their aunt dust the house and get the boys' bedroom ready for them. The time seemed to drag. All the work was finished by two o'clock.

"We have several hours before Ken and Chris arrive," Louise said. "I'm going to work on the markings that appear on both stelae and see if I can make anything out of them."

She went to her room and studied the intriguing designs for nearly two hours. The girl detective did not discover anything more than the Viking ships and the vertical and horizontal lines, which she thought were the initials of Leif Erikson.

In the meantime, Jean told the others she was going to stroll around the campus and think. "I hope I'll see or hear something that will give me some ideas about the missing codicil. I seem to have run dry."

She was gone over two hours, but finally returned without having gotten any new hunches. The Danas compared notes and felt a bit discouraged about the mystery.

Presently Jean shook her shoulders, leaned back, and gazed at the ceiling. "I won't admit defeat!" she declared. "Maybe after the boys arrive, they'll help us."

The girls assisted Aunt Betty with final preparations for dinner, then went upstairs to dress. Though the boys had said they would be there at about seven o'clock, both Louise and Jean began watching the grandfather clock in the first-floor hall from six thirty on.

At last it chimed the hour of seven. "Ken and Chris should be here any minute," Louise said, and Jean nodded. The sisters walked outside, ready to greet their friends.

Fifteen minutes went by, then another half

hour. Louise and Jean came back indoors. Both were worried.

"I suggest we eat dinner," Aunt Betty said. "Your uncle is starved and I'm sure you girls are hungry."

They all sat down. Grace was said and dinner was served. Louise and Jean suddenly found that they had little appetite for the delicious roast beef.

"Oh, come on and eat," Uncle Phil coaxed his nieces. "The boys may have had a flat tire or some minor mechanical failure, which tied them up. They should be along soon."

"I suppose so," Louise agreed. "But both Ken and Chris are so good about phoning when they're going to be late for a date. This isn't like them at all!"

Aunt Betty suggested that perhaps they were riding on country roads and could not reach a telephone along the way.

Louise and Jean knew their relatives were trying to comfort them, but they could not get the thought out of their minds that something had happened to the boys.

Finally, at nine o'clock, the telephone rang. Both girls rushed to answer it. "Hello! Hello!" they cried, excited.

The caller turned out to be Uncle Ned Dana. "My goodness, you girls sound terribly upset. What has happened?"

Louise told him that they were worried because Ken and Chris had not yet arrived for their seven o'clock date.

Uncle Ned chuckled. "Now, me hearties, stop your worries. They'll be along. They could have been tied up at an open bridge, or got caught in a parade, or—any number of things."

"It's sweet of you to try to comfort us," said Louise.

Captain Dana changed the subject. "I have some good news. You asked me in your cable to let you know what I could do about my ex-sailor Hoppy Canfield."

"Oh, yes," Jean said. "Are you going to be able to hire him again?"

"Well, that all depends," her uncle replied. "I'll withdraw my charges against the man. If the court dismisses the case and he has a clean record, he may come back to the *Balaska* and be reinstated."

"Oh, that's wonderful!" Louise exclaimed. "He's still in the hospital. We'll get word to him tomorrow."

There was little more conversation, then Uncle Ned said good-by, again asking the girls not to worry about Ken and Chris.

The Danas went at once to tell the Kenmores what Uncle Ned had agreed to do. The college president and his wife were delighted to hear that

Hoppy might be released and get his old job back. While they were talking, the phone rang again.

"Maybe that's Ken and Chris," Jean cried and beat her sister to the receiver by a fraction of a second.

CHAPTER XVII

An Explosion!

Louise and Jean sighed with relief when they heard the voices of Ken and Chris on the telephone. Both girls began to ask questions.

"Are you all right?"

"What happened to you?"

"Where are you?"

"Whoa!" Ken begged. "One question at a time, please."

As they talked, the girls realized that the boys were both weak and weary. They listened carefully as Ken explained what had happened to them. They had been in a bad car accident.

"We'd planned to get to your place early, but as we were coming along a country road, a car shot out of a hidden driveway and rammed into us!"

"Oh, how dreadful!" Jean exclaimed.

Louise added, "Are you sure you're all right?"

Chris tried to make light of the accident. "Sure we're all right. We have a few scratches and bruises, but nothing is broken."

The Danas learned that the boys' car was a complete wreck and they would not be able to go any farther that evening.

"We can't rent a car until morning," Ken explained. "Anyway, I think the two of us could do with a good night's sleep. We haven't had any supper because we spent a long time at the police station. They insisted that their surgeon give us a complete examination. We had lots of papers to fill out."

Louise asked what happened to the driver of the other car.

"Very little," Chris replied. "He must have fallen asleep at the wheel. I guess he was so relaxed that the bump didn't hurt him much. The police surgeon said he was okay, too, and wouldn't have to go to the hospital."

The boys said they would rent a car as soon as the agency opened. "We might even get to your place for breakfast!" Chris concluded.

"That would be great!" Jean exclaimed.

Both sisters expressed their relief and delight that the boys were all right, and said they would be waiting for them. The next morning Louise and Jean were up early and had started to prepare breakfast before their aunt and uncle came downstairs.

"Hm, something smells mighty good," Uncle Phil remarked. His eyes twinkled. "Am I to share in this, or is it just for the two young men who are coming?"

Jean screwed up her face. "Well, now, I'll tell you. If you'd like to sample what's cooking, we promise to give you a big portion."

The delicious aroma seemed to be coming from a good-sized raisin-and-cinnamon coffee cake, topped with brown-sugar icing.

By the time breakfast was ready, the front door-bell rang. Dr. Kenmore opened it. Ken and Chris stood there.

They introduced themselves, and the college president said, "Come in! We were very sorry to hear about your accident and the loss of your car."

By this time Louise and Jean hurried in from the kitchen and greeted their friends. Aunt Betty arrived and was introduced. Everyone wanted to hear more about the incident.

"As I told you on the phone," Ken said, "this fellow by the name of Joe Falcetano came out of a hidden driveway, disregarding a signal light. He rammed right into us. I'm sure he fell asleep behind the wheel."

"He looked positively exhausted," Chris added. "And he seemed very nervous, as if he were afraid someone might have followed him."

"Did you find out anything more about him?" Jean asked.

"No. The police made an accident report. Falcetano received a summons, then they let us all go."

"It certainly was tough luck," Dr. Kenmore remarked. "Maybe you boys would like to wash your hands, then we'll sit down to eat. My nieces have made a surprise for you."

"Great!" Ken said.

During the meal the boys were brought up-to-date on the hundred-year mystery. They learned about Lem, who had been discharged by Uncle Ned Dana, and his friend Hoppy, and how the girls had had a hand in getting Hoppy's job back for him. Ken and Chris also learned about the adventures the girls had had while trying to track down the lost codicil.

Aunt Betty said, "Let Louise tell you about her findings on the Viking design that appears on all our buildings and apparently was chosen by the founder, John Beacon."

"There's a meaning in it or a message?" Chris asked.

Louise nodded. "We think so, but we haven't quite figured it out."

As soon as everyone finished eating, the four young people walked outside and Louise pointed up at the series of Viking ships with the straight, vertical lines between them.

"I think they may be Leif Erikson's initials."

Ken whistled. "You've really deciphered something," he complimented her.

After showing the boys around the campus, Louise and Jean took them to the gazebo and pointed out the stela.

"There's a similar one down in the water," Jean told them. "It helped save Louise's and my lives."

"What do you mean?" Chris asked, concerned.

The sisters described their adventure in the water.

Chris shook his head as if he could not believe it. Then he said, "You girls must have more lives than a cat is supposed to. I'm sure you've used up more than nine with all the tight fixes you've been in."

Jean giggled and said, "Then it's a good thing I wasn't born a cat!"

Ken and Chris dropped to their knees and began to examine the design on the stela. Louise had just started to explain what she had discovered, when there was a sudden terrific explosion nearby. The concussion made the building tremble and swept the four young people off their feet. All of them were knocked to the floor.

Jean, however, had not been thrown flat. She was in a half-kneeling position, so that she could look out through one of the open sections of the gazebo. Though she was dazed, the young sleuth detected a man running away some distance from the gazebo. Within seconds he disappeared down the cliff.

It was a full minute before the young people

gathered their wits and were able to stand up again.

"What was it?" Ken asked.

Louise answered. "I don't know, but I suspect a bomb went off nearby."

Jean said, "I think I saw the person who planted it disappear down the cliff."

"Who was he?" Ken asked.

"I have no idea. He was running away fast and disappeared too quickly for me to identify him."

The young people hurried from the gazebo and went to look in the direction where Jean had seen the suspect. Near the edge of the cliff was a gaping hole where the bomb probably had been planted.

By this time people were running across the campus from all directions to see what had happened. In the foreground were Deb and Paul. Seeing Louise and Jean, they came up to them and asked what had gone off.

Before explaining, the girls introduced the couple to Ken and Chris, then Louise told them what little she knew. Everyone looked down the cliff but could see no one. They were puzzled.

Jean said, "Not enough time has gone by for anyone to reach the foot of the cliff. Where did that man go?"

Paul suggested that perhaps he had doubled back up the hill and disappeared across the campus. The three couples ran along the rim of the

Suddenly there was a terrific explosion!

cliff, looking in all directions. They saw no one.

Deb said, "We'll go to a phone and notify the police. I'm sure that man was part of some gang that is trying to keep us from finding the lost codicil."

She and Paul hurried off. The Danas told Ken and Chris about Peter T. Osterbridge, who seemed to be responsible for at least one of the tricks played on the Danas at the foot of the cliff.

"Obviously he works for Karpalow," Louise said. "I wouldn't be surprised if the man who just disappeared was Osterbridge."

"Too bad the police haven't caught him yet," Jean added.

In a few minutes, a group of workmen drove up in a truck, asking where the explosion had taken place and if anyone had been hurt.

The Danas told them that they had been in the gazebo at the time of the explosion and it had rocked.

"Perhaps it should be tested for stability," Jean added.

Soon afterward Dr. Kenmore arrived with two security guards. All three were greatly disturbed by what had happened. One guard immediately began to examine the area where the bomb had gone off, hunting for clues to the suspect. He found only tiny pieces of the exploded bomb wedged into the cliff.

Meanwhile, Dr. Kenmore talked with the Danas.

"This time I can't say you girls took any risky chances. This bombing was most unexpected. Nevertheless, it makes me wonder about the advisability of your continuing to try to solve our mystery."

"Oh, we wouldn't give it up now!" Jean exclaimed.

Louise added, "Uncle Phil, I think we must be getting near a solution, because our enemies appear to be desperate. We promise to stick together and look in all directions before proceeding with further investigations."

The college president looked at his nieces with admiration. "I must praise you for having real grit. All right. If you'll do as you say, I'll permit you to continue."

In a few moments he left, but while he had been talking to the girls, Ken and Chris had drawn closer to the cliff's edge and were gazing intently down the treacherous drop. When they returned to the girls, they said they were completely puzzled about where the suspect might have gone.

"I have one of my long hunches," Louise said.

"Let's hear it!" Ken begged.

Louise told them about the adventure the girls had had in the cave.

"Do you think the man knows of some other entrance to it?" Jean asked.

"Possibly," Louise replied. "There could be another secret tunnel from some point in the cliff or the hillside that leads to the cave we were in."

The others were astonished at Louise's guess but admitted it had merit.

"But we examined the cliff so thoroughly," Jean said thoughtfully.

"We might have missed it," Louise suggested. "If it's as well hidden as the cave entrance, the only way we could find it would be accidentally."

Chris was excited. "Let's try anyway!"

CHAPTER XVIII

The Stone Door

THE Danas and their friends were eager to follow Chris's suggestion and explore the cliff. They hoped fervently that they would find a secret entrance to a tunnel, which in turn would lead to the cave.

The young people stepped away from the gazebo, because the workmen were testing the stability of the structure.

"Let's go home first and freshen up," Louise suggested.

Jean agreed and added that she wanted to put on sturdier clothes than those she was wearing. "I can tell you boys from experience, the stony cliff is a rough place."

Louise said she also wanted to follow up a promise she had made. "I must telephone Hoppy at the hospital and tell him the good news from Uncle Ned." She turned to the boys and said,

"Captain Dana is willing to take him back on the ship."

As soon as they reached the Kenmore home, she put in the call. Hoppy said he was much improved and the doctor had told him he could probably leave in a few days. When he heard that there was a chance of his being rehired on the *Balaska*, he cried out with joy.

"I never should have left my ship in the first place," he said. "I love that old vessel."

Hoppy also said he had discussed his release with his detective-guard after Captain Dana had withdrawn the charges. The police chief had visited him personally and had had a long conversation with Hoppy.

"What was the outcome?" Louise asked.

The sailor said that an investigation showed no other charges had ever been made against him. As soon as the police received written word from Uncle Ned that he would not pursue the case and would reinstate Hoppy in his old job, the police would release him.

"The part you played in the scare tactics used against us will not be held against you?" Louise asked.

"No," Hoppy answered. "I didn't do anything destructive and didn't really hurt anyone."

The girl detective now asked him if he had heard from his friend Lem.

Hoppy said no. Apparently his former buddy had no idea where Hoppy was.

"Do you know whether the police have any leads to Karpalow?" Louise asked.

"According to my guard, they have no clues," he answered.

Louise promised to get in touch with Hoppy again before he left the hospital. Then she hung up and went back to Jean and the boys.

She told them of her conversation with the sailor, and ended with a sigh. "We have so much to do. We must find Karpalow and Lem and locate either the missing codicil or the treasure hinted at in the will."

Jean said, "You're right. It almost seems as if we're back where we started from."

"Oh, come now," Ken urged. "It's not that bad. You have Chris and me all excited about a new lead. Let's get started as soon as we can."

"You're right!" Jean agreed. "As soon as we change our clothes, we'll get a couple of lanterns, and start off."

On their way to the section of the cliff they planned to descend, the two couples stopped at the gazebo. The workmen were just getting ready to leave. They told the young people that the place was once more sound and safe to be in. They were glad to hear this.

The four went beyond the end of the fence,

then started down. At first both Ken and Chris began to slide precariously.

"Dig in!" Louise warned.

Jean added, "Louise and I learned that the hard way when we went down before. Take a zigzag course."

Soon the boys got the knack of descending the cliff without slipping. They had gone about half-way down without seeing anything that might be the entrance to another secret cave. There were no large clumps of bushes anywhere.

While circling the face of the cliff, Ken had put some distance between himself and the others. Suddenly he cried out, "I think I've found something!"

The others hurried toward him as fast as they could. Ken had seen a fairly large outcrop of rock, which he decided to dislodge. After a great deal of effort, he had managed to loosen it and the stones had gone rolling down the cliff.

"Look!" he exclaimed, pointing.

To the others' amazement, he had discovered a narrow, man-made tunnel. The Dana girls and Chris were as excited as Ken himself. Jean started to squeeze herself into the opening, but Chris pulled her back.

"That's too tight. There may not be a place to turn around and you might have to wriggle all the way back."

Ken agreed with him and suggested that the two boys go in first and see what they could find.

"If the place is safe and large enough to get in and out of comfortably, we'll come back and get you girls."

"All right," Louise said, "but please don't be long and leave Jean and me to worry ourselves sick over you as we did when you had that auto accident."

Ken grinned, "I'm sure nothing's going to run into us in this place," he said, "unless there's a snake or two around."

The girls made faces but said no more. Holding his lantern ahead of him, Ken wriggled into the opening first, and Chris followed.

Jean turned to her sister. "Louise, this isn't like us. We never let anything stop us when we have a good clue."

Louise agreed, but said no doubt the boys would be back soon and then the girls would know what to do.

As the minutes went by, the young sleuths grew restless. Because the side of the cliff was steep, there was no place for them to walk up and down to calm their nerves. They had left their wrist-watches at home, so they had no way of telling what time it was or how many minutes had passed.

Once Jean went to the opening in the cliff and called, "Chris! Ken!"

There was no reply.

A few minutes later, Louise did the same thing with the same result. Both girls tried shouting together, but all they got was the hollow echo of their voices.

The Danas sat down but never took their eyes off the spot where the boys had crawled inside. A little while later they thought they heard a noise. Both of them looked around, but no one was in sight! Again they riveted their eyes on the entrance. Then they exclaimed in surprise.

A skeleton was dangling from the opening!

Next Ken crawled out. He was holding up the bony frame, as Chris followed.

"Here's your lost friend!" Ken said.

"You found him in there?" Louise said. "Did you come across a connection to the cave?"

Ken replied yes to the first question, and no to the second one. "The skeleton was the only thing we discovered. You'll have to figure out how it got there."

"Maybe it's not the same one," Chris suggested.

Louise looked at it carefully. "Yes, it is," she said. "See this little depression in the skull? The one we saw in the cave was identical."

Ken told the Danas that it was of no use for them to waste time going inside. "The place does widen enough so you can turn around, but it's very uncomfortable," he said.

Jean declared that there had to be some opening

between this tunnel and the cave. There was no other way that the skeleton could have been removed from one and taken to the other while the girls were in the cave.

"Then why are we standing here?" Louise asked. "Let's go back to the cave and hunt for a breakthrough in there."

Ken suggested that they pace off an estimated distance along the side of the cliff, where the two underground passages might meet. The boys did this, then the young people went on with the skeleton.

On the way they met Deb and Paul, who stopped in surprise. "Where did you find our elusive buddy," Deb asked.

The couple was told, and the Danas also explained what they and their friends hoped to accomplish.

"What are you going to do with this heap of bones?" Paul asked.

Louise admitted they had not discussed the subject, but said, "How would you like to take him to Dr. Kenmore's house for us?"

Deb giggled and agreed to run the errand. Paul took the skeleton and swung it over his shoulder. With everyone laughing at the strange sight, the couple walked away.

The others set off at once to the big clump of bushes that hid the entrance to the large cave. They held the sturdy growth aside and went in.

With the help of their lanterns, the four inspected every inch of the rock wall. There was no sign of any opening!

"Stymied again!" Chris said in disgust.

"What do we do now?" Ken wanted to know.

At first no one answered him but finally Jean spoke. "I have been wondering why the person who set the skeleton in the cave put him in that particular spot. Maybe it was meant as a marker for an opening."

They walked to the area, and examined the craggy walls inch by inch.

Suddenly Jean gave a gleeful cry. "Here's a large, well-concealed iron ring among these stones. And look! I'd say there is cement between the crevices."

"Which means," Louise said, "that there might be a door here leading into the other cave."

"Exactly," Jean replied. "Help me pull on this ring and see what happens."

The four searchers grabbed the ring and yanked hard. At first nothing happened, but after several hefty pulls a stone door opened. On the other side of it lay another cave!

Ken offered to crawl through it to be sure this was the one the boys had discovered. "I'll meet you at the top of the cliff," he said, and began his journey.

As the others watched him go, Louise said, "We've solved the mystery of the missing skeleton, but we don't have a single clue to the missing codicil."

"We'll find one," Chris said hopefully.

He and the girls closed the door and went back to the entrance of the cave and up to the rim of the cliff. In a short time they saw Ken emerge from the hole he had discovered earlier at the side of the cliff. He climbed up and met them.

"It's the same cave," he told the others. "And I don't mind saying I'm ready to go home and take a good bath!"

When they reached the Kenmore house, no one was there, so the four young people had a chance to make themselves more presentable before Dr. and Mrs. Kenmore came in.

The couple was intrigued by the story of the two caves. Aunt Betty said, "Deb and Paul brought us the skeleton. He put it down in the basement for me. Tomorrow you folks should take it to our medical laboratory for further research on its age, racial background, and so on."

"I'll do it," Uncle Phil offered.

The following morning Louise greeted everyone with excitement in her eyes. She had a new and stronger hunch about where the missing codicil or the treasure might be.

"Something I read gave me the idea. I think the clue will be found in one or the other of the stelae. Since one of them is partially covered with water sometimes, and entirely submerged the rest of the day, why don't we work on the one in the gazebo?"

When the Danas and their friends arrived at the attractive open-air building, they began to study the design on the stela intently.

Both boys declared they could make nothing more out of it than what Louise had told them. Jean, too, said she was at a loss. All eyes turned to Louise.

"Have you figured anything out yet?" Jean asked her.

Before answering, Louise counted on her fingers. The others wondered why she was doing this. After going over the same numbers several times, she exclaimed, "I think I have it! I'm sure I know now where the treasure was buried. An old Viking formula was used!"

CHAPTER XIX

The Secret Pit

JUST as Louise finished making her astounding announcement, the group was joined by Paul and Deb. Louise told them she had figured out a formula from the distances on the gazebo's stela, based on her recent reading about the Vikings. The measurements between the symbols were different from those in the other building decorations she had observed.

"That's strange and interesting," Deb remarked. "How are they different?"

Everyone gathered around the young sleuth as she pointed out the ships and the E L around the top of the stone post.

"Notice that these are well separated, while the figures in all the other places I've seen are set close together. I read about an old Viking method of burying their treasures, which could be indicated here."

As Louise paused, Ken urged her to go on. "Don't stop now," he begged. "How do you interpret the distances?"

Louise pointed out that the measurement between the two ships standing stern to stern was just the same. "The next separation from the ship to what I think is an L is exactly the same," she went on. "But the L and the E are a little farther apart on this stela."

Paul said, "Granted that this is true, what does it mean?"

"The ancient Vikings," Louise began, "used to bury things at specific levels. According to one account I read, a favorite formula of theirs was five, five, and seven. The first burial level was approximately five feet down, the next one below it another five feet, and the third one seven feet blow the second."

"That's amazing!" Deb exclaimed.

The boys wanted to know what separated the layers. Louise told them that sometimes it was a wooden platform; at other times something from the area they were in was used.

"In other words," Jean said, "if we dig down here to the five-foot level we may find a large stone slab."

Louise nodded and Jean went on, "And at the next five foot level we'll find a similar one, and then seven feet below that we'll hit the bottom."

All eyes turned to Louise. Her own were dancing with excitement. "If I'm right, I believe the treasure willed to Beacon College will be waiting for us!"

"But how do you know a five-five-seven formula was used by John Beacon?" Jean asked. "It could be three-three-five, or a million other combinations."

"True," Louise admitted. "But if this is the correct spot, the first platform will indicate the first number, and the second one will be the same, and the third one will be slightly deeper."

"Well, what are we waiting for?" Paul called out. "Shouldn't we get going with the digging?"

Louise and Jean insisted that Dr. Kenmore be notified before they tore anything up. Deb and Paul offered to rush over to the administration building to get him. In a short time the three of them arrived in his car.

The college president was thunderstruck to hear the latest development in the mystery. Quickly Louise reiterated her reason for thinking they might find a treasure buried seventeen feet down. At once he became enthusiastic and began to give orders.

"Paul, you rush off and get several more boys to come and help with the digging."

Over his car radio, which Dr. Kenmore used to communicate with any building on campus, he ordered picks and shovels as well as the college-owned digging machine.

Within half an hour Ken, Chris, Paul, and several other boys were hard at work. First they dug down around the stela, which was deep in the soil. Finally they were able to drag it out.

Paul remarked, "If John Beacon buried that himself, I'd say he was a pretty hefty man."

Jean reminded him that apparently Beacon had engineered the digging of the whole pit. "I don't see how he could have done the work alone, but if he wanted to keep it a strict secret, how would he dare let anyone assist him?"

The boys were too busy to think of an answer to this question. They worked in a circle. With the help of students they soon had a sizeable amount of dirt and stones piled up inside the gazebo. The girls watched eagerly, the Danas itching to have some part in the exciting work.

Jean whispered her desires to her sister, then said, "Louise, this whole idea was yours. So you had the bigger part in it. As for me, I have done nothing."

"Don't worry," Louise said to her. "We haven't been at this job very long. You may get a chance yet."

It seemed no time at all before the diggers reached the five-foot level.

Chris was the first one to cry out, "Here is a great big stone slab!"

Louise was thrilled and relieved. She would

have felt very foolish if her hunch had been wrong and all the digging had been for nothing.

The stone slab was extremely heavy, and again the onlookers wondered how John Beacon could possibly have put it there by himself. They were more and more convinced that he had had help. Since no one had come forward to tell the secret, it was assumed that any assistants had also died without revealing the secret.

The digging machine was now brought into action. The boys climbed topside, and then the operator of the digger turned on his motor. The great claws of his shovel swung on a crane through the broad entrance of the gazebo and into the hole.

Quickly it scooped up the dirt and deposited it on the ground above. Louise and Jean had moved outside the gazebo with Deb so they would not be hit with the boom from the crane when it pulled up and swung the shovel around.

Presently Dr. Kenmore suggested, "We'd better carry the extra earth outside the gazebo." The boys got busy with buckets from the truck to do this.

Within a few minutes the great claws reached the second five-foot level. The shovel was brought to the surface and the motor stopped. The operator announced that the hole was now about ten feet deep.

Louise said, "Uncle Phil, don't you think one of us should go down and find out if there is another platform of some sort there?"

Dr. Kenmore agreed and asked Paul to drive to the college's maintenance department and ask them to bring a long ladder. Fifteen minutes later, with all the workers eager to learn the truth, the ladder arrived. Two men lowered the long ladder into the hole.

"What do you want us to look for?" one of them asked.

Dr. Kenmore was reluctant to spread the secret, so he said, "Oh, just hold the ladder tight. One of the boys will go down."

Several students jumped forward, but Ken was in the lead and was the first to descend. In a few minutes he was back up. All he said was, "I think it's okay to continue with the work."

"All right," the college president answered.

The man in charge of the digger said that his equipment would not go down more than ten feet.

Dr. Kenmore asked the maintenance men if they had long ropes on their truck.

"We sure do, sir," one replied.

When he brought them over Chris asked, "How long are the ropes?"

"About fifty feet," the man replied.

"Just leave everything," Dr. Kenmore said. "I'll let you know when to come for it." The men hopped aboard the vehicle and drove off.

Next, the college president told the operator of the digger he would not use him any longer, so he too went clattering away.

Ken, Chris, Paul, and one other boy took shovels and descended the ladder. A fifth boy, carrying a strong searchlight, followed, beaming it below.

Louise was impatient to hear what they would find. She called down into the hole, "Do you see anything?"

"Another stone slab," Ken replied. "Don't ask me how we're ever going to get it out of here."

"Maybe you won't have to," Louise said. "Couldn't you just turn it up on end?"

"We'll try," Ken answered.

There was no more talking for a while. Finally Louise, by straining her eyes, could see that the boys had accomplished this. To everyone's amazement they were standing on a narrow, earth-and-stone bridge, which extended from one side of the second level to the other.

The spaces on each flank of the bridge were hollow with inky blackness below. Louise suddenly realized that the boys were in a precarious spot!

"You'd better get up here as fast as possible!" she warned.

Either the boys did not hear her or paid no

attention for several minutes. Then Paul called up, "It's perfectly safe, but we need the ropes."

One by one all the boys except Ken climbed the ladder.

"Why didn't Ken come?" Louise asked fearfully.

Paul said that the little bridge seemed to be solid and evidently had been left there as a support for the heavy stone slab.

"What did you see below the ten-foot level?" Jean prodded.

"Not much," he replied. "If the section below two or three feet was clear originally, some of the sides have caved in and covered up whatever is buried there," Paul replied.

The ladder was not long enough to go down another seven feet, and it seemed best to leave it in place as an escape route if the ropes failed. The group at the top discussed what their next move should be. They decided to climb down from the second level by using the ropes. As they removed the dirt, at the rim the watchers would slacken the ropes and wind the ends around one of the sturdy pillars of the gazebo.

"All ready!" Dr. Kenmore called out. "And do be careful!"

Two ropes had been dropped into the pit. Jean looked at a third one and said, "I don't see any reason why I can't go down there and help!"

Her uncle looked at her and smiled. "Okay! Go ahead!"

One by one the boys descended the ladder. When each of them reached the bridge, he transferred to the rope and lowered himself into the black pit. When everyone was down, the boys asked Jean to take charge of the buckets of soil to be pulled to the surface.

Those at the top became so busy dumping the buckets of earth outside the gazebo that they did not notice any outsiders looking on.

Louise called down into the ever-deepening hole and asked loudly, "What's happening?"

Her sister cupped her hands around her mouth and shouted up, "We're almost at the seven-foot level! Oh, it's so exciting!"

At this moment, with no warning of any kind, a powerful stream of water suddenly hit those in the gazebo. As they turned to see what had occurred, they were almost blinded by a second gush of water. It was spurting in all directions at once so there was no chance to escape it. The force of water was so strong that it knocked Louise and Deb off balance.

Dr. Kenmore held his hand across his face and was trying to see where the water was coming from. Already soaked he staggered from side to side, trying to avoid the deluge.

Louise had jumped over a rear railing of the

gazebo and finally scooted out of the path of the water. Now, not far away, she could see a man at the nearby fire hydrant. With one hand he was holding a hose and with the other he was turning a wheel on the hydrant to increase the force of the flow. The man had switched the nozzle of the hose to a spray.

As quickly as she could, Louise crept around the side of the gazebo and crossed a grassy plot. She realized that if she shouted at the man, he probably could not hear her from so far away.

"I'll just have to get closer!" the young sleuth decided.

Louise ran and finally was within earshot of the man near the hydrant. "Stop that!" she shouted. "Turn off that water!"

The man, who had shaggy hair and wore a shaggy beard, evidently heard her.

He turned and yelled at the top of his lungs, "You tell Dr. Kenmore to make the deal with me right away and give me the hundred thousand dollars, or I'll drown everyone down in that hole!"

CHAPTER XX

Amazing Discovery

By this time several other students had come by to find out what was going on. When they heard the ultimatum of the man wielding the fire hose, they were horrified.

Louise kept yelling at him to turn off the water. He paid no attention and sneered at her. "You won't get the best of me! Nobody can. Anyone who comes near me will get soaked and hurt from the force of this water!"

Quickly Louise conferred with some of the boys standing around. She asked them if they would sneak up behind the stranger and capture him.

"Then turn off the water!" she added.

The students attempted to do this, but the man was not about to be trapped. He circled in every direction and let the water soak all those within its reach.

Then suddenly he laid down the hose, turned the stream directly toward the gazebo, and ran like mad to the cliff. He was tackled by the two boys who were closest to him, but with almost superhuman strength he shook both of them loose.

Meanwhile another student rushed to the hydrant and tried to shut off the water. To his dismay the wheel was stuck. "This will need a wrench to free it," he said. "What'll we do now?"

"Turn the hose away from the gazebo," Louise replied. "Then go after the man. If enough people fan out on the cliff, he can't go anywhere but down. I'll call the police."

As she ran toward the telephone, which she had used so often in the last few days, Louise became alarmed about her sister and the boys trapped in the pit.

"I hope they'll get out all right," she prayed, trusting they could climb the ropes.

Louise dialed police headquarters, and told the sergeant on duty what had happened.

"The man is going down the cliff," she said. "There are two secret caves in the side of the cliff but I doubt that he'll have time to squeeze into either one. Besides, a lot of people are chasing him and keeping an eye on him. If you could send a police launch—"

"Will do," the sergeant said. "By the way, I

heard a hose was stolen from Fire Station No. Three. That must be the one the guy used."

Next Louise called the maintenance men and asked them to bring a wrench and turn off the hydrant. Then she ran back to the gazebo.

Dr. Kenmore meanwhile had been issuing orders. The boys standing around the pit were to pull up the ropes supporting the trapped workers to the base of the ladder, then the workers were to climb to the surface as quickly as possible.

Louise returned just in time to see her muddy, water-soaked sister emerge from the pit. She rushed to her.

"Are you all right?" she asked.

Jean looked angry. "Who put all that water down in the pit?"

Louise quickly explained what had happened, and Jean cried out, "Do you think it was Karpalow?"

Louise said she thought it was, because he had demanded the hundred thousand dollars, and she was sure the man was half demented. "You should have heard the snarl in his voice when he threatened to drown all of you!"

Jean said, "It looks as if he's at the end of the line. Nobody in his right mind would stand out in the open like a target and risk capture."

"Speaking of capture, I wonder how the police are doing," Louise said.

At this moment Ken appeared at the top of the

ladder. He too was water-soaked and muddy. He asked Louise what had happened. The other two boys followed, and Louise gave them a quick report. Then all went to the rim of the cliff to see how the chase was progressing.

Louise saw the stranger approaching the bottom. Several students were close behind him, and as he reached the shoreline, a police launch pulled up. The culprit tried to run to the right, but two young people, who were on that side to block him, chased him back. The same thing happened when he tried the left. He was trapped!

"They've got him!" Louise exclaimed happily when an officer snapped handcuffs on the fugitive.

A shout of joy went up from all the young people as the man was led onto the launch.

Meanwhile the hydrant had been turned off. When the Dana group returned to the gazebo, Dr. Kenmore said, "The water in the pit will have to be pumped out before you can proceed with your work. Why don't you go home and take showers and relax. I've already called the fire department and they'll be here shortly with a pump."

"Okay," Louise said, looking at her soggy clothes. "We'll be glad to."

Everyone hurried off. As soon as Louise had had a shower and shampoo, and put on fresh clothing, she hurried downstairs and called the police department. She asked Sergeant Thomas if they had a confession from their prisoner.

"I'll switch you to the chief," the sergeant told her.

"We've caught the fellow, thanks to you," the chief told her. "He gave us a full confession. Said he was using the name Karpalow to avoid detection, but his real name is Wilson. He escaped from a mental institution a while ago. We'll return him immediately."

"Did he mention his confederates?" Louise asked.

"Yes. He had a pal named Osterbridge, as you already know. We've arrested him, too. Karpalow told us where to find him."

"Great. And how does Lem fit into the picture?"

"He's a distant cousin of Karpalow's. My men are bringing him in right now."

"I wonder if he stole the manuscript from the library," Louise said.

"No. Karpalow did. But he let his buddies do most of the dirty work. Lem let loose a fer-de-lance snake for him; Osterbridge threw a rock at you and set off the bomb. The note written to Dr. Kenmore from the so-called ex-caretaker came from another pal of Karpalow's.

"Later, he had a falling out with Karpalow when he disagreed with Karpalow's ruthless methods. So he wrote the note, but then made the mistake of telling Karpalow about it. Karpalow got violent and he ran."

"How did Karpalow know about the codicil?" Louise asked the chief.

"He heard the story from another patient in the mental institution. When he escaped, he went to New York and talked to Lem. Then he came back here and looked up his childhood friend Peter Osterbridge.

"Pete offered his help in the extortion scheme, and soon afterwards Lem and Hoppy Canfield arrived on the scene."

"Amazing," Louise said. "Now I understand the whole thing. Only one point hasn't been cleared up, yet—the skeleton."

"Oh!" The police chief laughed. "I heard about that, too. You see, Karpalow and Osterbridge knew about the caves from the time they were kids and used to play on the cliff. The skeleton had been in there long before that. When you people explored the larger cave, Osterbridge was in the smaller one and heard you. He got worried and wanted to scare you. Figuring you'd be back, probably with reinforcements, he removed Mr. Bones so you'd get scared and stay away from there."

Louise laughed. "He didn't succeed!" She thanked the chief and reported the whole story to Jean and the Kenmores.

Everyone was delighted that this part of the mystery was solved, and that at last they could make a further search without being annoyed or endangered during their hunt.

By the time Louise, Jean, Chris, and Ken returned to the gazebo, the firemen had pumped all the water out of the pit and forced air in to dry it.

Louise turned to her Uncle Phil. "Please, now may we go down and investigate?"

He smiled. "All right, but take it easy. I'll be standing right here at the edge to hear what you discover."

In a few minutes Deb and Paul joined the other four and they too went below. There was not enough standing room at the lowest level for the entire team of diggers, so a relay was set up near the ladder. As soon as one group tired, the other would spell it.

"I think we've hit rocks," Chris remarked presently. "What do we do now?"

Louise beamed her strong light directly on the earth. "I don't think this is rock," she said. "I believe we've hit a box!"

The diggers went to work with renewed effort. In a few minutes they had unearthed a large stone chest.

"We'll never be able to lift this out of the pit," Ken said. "The best thing to do is open it right here."

There seemed to be a lid but no way to lift it, and no lock of any kind was visible.

Jean called up to those waiting by the ladder and said, "Ask Dr. Kenmore to come down here! Tell him we think we've found the treasure!"

The college president reached the bottom of the pit quickly. He gazed at the stone chest. "Amazing! Absolutely amazing!" he remarked.

Chris asked, "Have you any suggestion about how to open this?"

Dr. Kenmore examined the object carefully, then remarked, "I believe the top is a stone slab and that there is no lock on the chest."

At once he, Ken, and Chris tried to raise the lid. At first they seemed to make no progress, but suddenly it moved sideways a fraction of an inch.

"We have it!" Ken exclaimed.

Louise suggested that maybe the cover slid open sideways and not upward.

"If so, we'll have to dig around it," Chris said.

They used picks on each side of the lid. Presently they found that some earth and small stones were giving way. They dug furiously and brought out several shovelfuls of dirt.

Now Dr. Kenmore and the two boys shoved the heavy stone lid to one side. It moved more easily than they had suspected it might.

"Look! Here's a cleverly constructed groove through which it moves!" Ken pointed out.

Suddenly the whole lid slid back. Jean exclaimed, "The treasure! We've found it!"

Inside the oblong stone chest, which was about two feet wide, three long and three deep, lay a large collection of priceless old jewelry. There was also a large quantity of coins and several valuable swords.

Dr. Kenmore had not spoken for several minutes. He stared at the heap before him as if mesmerized. Finally he said, "It is a treasure, indeed! I would guess that the contents of this stone chest is worth a million dollars!"

Louise asked, "May I look at some of the pieces?"

"Go ahead."

She rummaged through the pile, holding up one exquisite piece after another. Finally she reached down to the bottom of the chest. A puzzled look came over her face as she put in her other hand and pushed aside the jewels and coins. Then she drew up several folded sheets, which she handed to Dr. Kenmore.

"I assume these belong to you," she said. "But do let us hear if there is anything written on them."

Dr. Kenmore spread out the first sheet and asked Jean to beam a strong light on it. At the top he read, "Draft of a codicil to be put with my will."

Excited, he read that the Viking treasure had been kept a family secret for many years. The

Beacons were not related to Leif Erikson, but to his first mate.

Their ship had indeed been badly damaged on the rocks of Still Harbor. Leif Erikson had put the stela in the bay himself, while the crew were repairing the ship and getting ready to sail back to Norway.

The rough draft of the codicil went on to say that Erikson's first mate was an Englishman, with a Viking mother. His name was John Beacon and the name had come down through his family since Viking days.

"Amazing!" Jean said. "This is just fabulous."

"Wait until you hear what's next," her uncle said. "It says that the original John Beacon had not remained on the *Thor* but had gone back to England. He had been given his share of the loot before leaving Still Harbor, and had buried it in a cave above the stela Erikson had sunk into the harbor."

"The treasure was probably stolen from all over the world," Chris said with a chuckle.

Dr. Kenmore nodded and read on, " 'I believe that when the college has its centennial celebration most of the money will have been used up, and the old Viking treasure will be needed.' "

Dr. Kenmore smiled. "And old John Beacon was right!"

He read more. Then he said, "The secret of the

treasure chest was handed down to the oldest son in each generation. Around 1500, John Beacon, a direct descendant who knew the secret decided to come to America and look for the treasure. He unearthed the chest. Then because he had plenty of money, he decided not to use the treasure, but to hand down the secret as his ancestors had done."

Uncle Phil paused for a moment, then read a section of the codicil aloud. " 'The family has shrunk until only I am left. I am a bachelor and have decided to leave my money and the Viking treasure to found a college. I will bury the chest as my ancient ancestors often did, and put a code on the stela I will erect on the ground above it.' "

Jean remarked, "I guess the gazebo was built over the stela later. Mr. Beacon doesn't say anything about it in this paper."

"You're right," her uncle replied. "It was erected about fifty years ago."

Deb spoke up. "John Beacon probably never did get around to making a finished copy of this codicil and giving it to his lawyers. In his diary he said he had injured himself burying the treasure."

"And he buried it deep," Ken remarked.

Louise and Jean suddenly realized that the hundred-year-old mystery had been solved. When would another come their way? Very soon and it would be called *Mountain-Peak Mystery*.

As the little group at the bottom of the pit gazed at the treasure, Dr. Kenmore remarked, "Actually it wasn't necessary for us to find the codicil. The directions weren't needed. My wonderful young detective nieces, Louise and Jean Dana, figured out where the old Viking treasure was!"